Toby Weston (born May 8th
and technologist.

His work weaves action and philosophy while dealing
with the themes of consciousness, utopia, and the
technological singularity.

His books are grounded in science, but he is prepared to
take excursions into the fantastic.

Before writing books, Toby worked as a parking attendant, spook, tour guide, software engineer and chef (if
you count making sandwiches).

His academic background spans Software Engineering,
Computational Neuroscience, Environmental Biology
and Deep Learning.

He is currently based in Switzerland where he writes and
works in the field of digital innovation.

Singularity's Children

Book Two

Disruption

By
Toby Weston

LOBSTER

Copyright

Published by
Lobster Books

ISBN 978-0995515819

2.0

Many Thanks Ke

CONTENTS

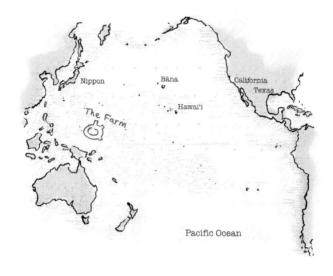

Nippon   Bāna   California
Hawai'i   Texas

The Farm

Pacific Ocean

A glossary of technologies and locations from the books and a full
dramatis personæ of characters is available at:

www.tobyweston.net/members

Preface

The Earth of this book is not ours;
it's a butterfly flap away.

This is not important. It is mostly a literary device to allow the author lenience with dates and with histories past and future.

Mostly.

"Growth for the sake of growth is the ideology of the cancer cell."

Edward Abbey

A sponge, arguably the first creature to build its body from more than a single cell, is barely an *'it'* at all. What appears as one organism, is better described as a semi-autonomous collective. A host of loosely cooperating individuals building a shambling whole. Force a sponge through a fine sieve and the cloud of cells will happily reform, members taking on new roles, while the whole reassembles anew.

The minds of humans are similarly a curious assembly of barely integrated parts. Fossilised cognitive impressions of the Lizard and the Mouse contest with the many archetypes of the Man for control. Viewing through the same physical eyes, each facet of the self sees the world from a different perspective. The lizards and mice scurrying around inside our skulls want to fuck and flee. They live for the now. Complex arguments are lost on them, yet those nervous little animals dominate our emotions, give us our *joie de vivre,* and make our hearts race with terror or lust.

Sitting in there, among the dashing rodents and skulking reptiles, are patient academics scrutinising the world's patterns; planning, preparing, and bickering.

The din of voices within grows so loud it penetrates the honeycomb soundproofing of the skull, allowing the inadequacies, cognitive blind spots and perversions of the sub-ego choir to escape to echo across society.

The din drowns out the voices of the few enlightened individuals who have their own internal vermin under control. The rutting, racist majority, whose hyperbolic discount functions force inactivity in the face of anything but the most immediate pressing crises, run the show. The result is a massive drunken stagger, a comical lurching lunge across a darkened, danger-strewn globe.

Ignorance and idiocy—with a last-minute frosting of genius—create our familiar anarchy perpetually balanced on the verge of catastrophic Armageddon.

***

Keith tried to stay focused as the last hundred years of European and colonial succession were dissected and splayed on the 3D screens. The revolutions that decapitated the Ottoman and Russ empires in 1911; the fall of the Holy Empire in 1928; the new, straight lines that so disastrously redrew Europe in 1956 after the World War; the inevitable fragmentation and civil war from Kabul to Kitzbul, when the era of state power entered its twilight years; finally, the creeping spread of the Islamic Caliphate which, by 2030, stretched in one green block from Pakistan to Morocco. The accelerated history illuminated the growth and decay of states and their dogma, giving the appearance of organic living things, pulsing their colours across its surface like amoebae battling in a petri dish.

The perceived needs, dictated by the menagerie of pre-sentient, pseudo-personalities, motivated men to kill and take—or, more often, motivated leaders to command others to kill, take and deliver.

This was the mess Keith and his new chums would live in. Tasked by the populist, furiously optimistic, UK Forward Government with the patently impossible task of maintaining a crumbling imperial remnant against a growing list of fourth-generation actors: distributed republics, criminal cartels, trading bots, and pseudo-states. Old survivors, like the newly resurrected Caliphate or the Catholic Church, were also playing again, despite having sat out whole turns of the game. After languishing for a thousand years, they had shuddered and grabbed the dice, jumping from parchment, past industrialisation, directly to ad hoc distributed meshes of power, information and reputation.

The vivid reds, blues, and greens violated Keith's sensitive retinas. His head hurt, and not just from last night's Absinthe. It was a fucking nightmare. All over the map, people were killing each other, ostensibly for vague esoteric reasons involving gods or ancient wrongs; but, from the maps and charts, it was clear they were fighting for the scraps left on the table after the party had moved on.

The Captain barked again.

'At ease' meant standing more erect than Keith's most puffed-up preening.

'Attention!' implied unobtainable levels of verticality.

The base was thirty kilometres outside Prague. A strange, fungal cluster of bulging tumours embedded in an onion of razor wire. The bombproof structures were poured from a mix of concrete and carbon fibre into hollow inflated forms that, once the concrete had solidified, were removed to leave buildings like unfortunate stranded jellyfish. The cluster was built on a low hill that protruded from the surrounding pine forest. Streaked and weathered, stained variously piss yellow or puke green, the bulbous structures looked sick.

Keith felt sick. Sick of the army that had finally caught up with him after stalking him patiently for most of his life. It had been like some ever-present, lurking predator. As money and hope ran low, it had sensed weakness and crept closer. He'd managed to put some distance between him and it when he had gone to work for Ben and his father, but that period of relative affluence had ended shortly after he violently assaulted his boss in a jungle bar. The Business Class flight back to London had been his last taste of corporate nipple. Official termination papers had been waiting at his apartment, and so began his unenthusiastic slide into itinerancy.

After months of couch surfing, serially exhausting the hospitality of his remaining friends, options had persistently failed to materialise. His support network had become a dying camp fire, a fragile contracting circle of light, unable in its diminished state to hold back the hunters in the night. As patience and money had run out, the old nemesis had crept in. Keith, weak, out of options, unable to protest, had felt it close cold jaws around his leg, then watched, as if disembodied, while it dragged him out of the firelight to join hundreds of other disillusioned young men with similar stories.

The familiarity of his new life had been the first shock. Stand up, sit down, drop and give me twenty. It was public school again: discipline, achievement and unflinching obedience. Keith at least knew the rules of the game, unlike some of the other unfortunate victims, who were still reeling from the novelty of informal hazing and officially sanctioned violence.

Geopolitics over for the day, their brains were granted a fifteen-minute reprieve to replenish stimulant levels. Keith filtered out of the lecture hall with the others. Coffee was available. He took an aluminium beaker and went to stand in the drizzle with his new friends from the north end of the long dormitory. Most were smoking. Jones, the obligatory Welsh boy, was enduring some gentle racial abuse from Sten, a wiry cockney of East African descent. Keith cupped his beaker in both hands and sipped the astringent liquid.

"What's next?" he asked.

The others, happy to turn away from what had become a predictable exchange of racial stereotypes, acknowledged Keith's arrival with nods and grunts. He was ten years older than most, which translated to a perceived seniority, and he was usually left out of their primate social jostling.

"IEDs and shit," Jones replied.

"Yeah. One million and one ways to die in the East," someone added.

"We're heading off-base again tonight. You coming, Special?" Sten asked Keith.

"Yeah, why not? Might be the last chance for a while."

"Why'd you say that?" Jones asked.

"They don't grant this many passes, unless we are gearing up, right K?" one of the others offered.

"Yeah, that's probably how it works," Keith replied. "After

three nights on the town in Prague, we'll all have hangovers so big that house-to-house in a bombed-out ghost town will feel like a spa weekend."

Cigarettes were toked upon and coffee sipped as these words of wisdom were digested. The soon-to-be soldiers were lost in themselves. Six months of training were coming to an end. It had been hard. Two months ago, the brutal repetitive physical programme of the Aberdeen base had transitioned into a mix of drills, lectures and exercises on kit, tech, and vehicles. Three weeks ago, they had moved to their current home, out on the edge of Europe. More squads were arriving each day.

Sleek, silent, almost invisible VTOL attack drones slid over the fence at all hours, returning with little fanfare, to be refuelled and rearmed and sent back out. At least once a night, one of the ancient noisy tiltrotors thundered off from the other end of the base, carrying men to do work too dirty for machines.

A flat-sounding buzzing announced playtime was over, prompting cigarettes to be crushed and dregs to be flung out onto the parade ground.

The rest of the morning passed in a blur of DNA-triggered charges, high-altitude glider-launched kinetic energy impactors, assassin snake-bots, and dozens of other novel and interesting toys the Surgies had cooked up to kill them. Tomorrow would be software attacks. The instructor had happily informed them that firmware hacks to their own weapons systems were the most apparent threat, accounting for as many deaths as roadside bombs.

Cabbage, potato and what was allegedly pork were piled on Keith's plate, lashed with a brown, viscous, salty goop. Even the catering seemed to be run according to the same system as his school.

The recruits sat on pine benches, morosely looking at their plates, the table, or their fingers. Cold bodies dressed in drab olive, hair shorn to the scalp, rings under the eyes from exhaustion. Callouses on hands from a surprising, and likely pointless, amount of rope climbing.

"Cabbage!"

"Calm down, Burt. Let's not have another flare-up isn't it!" Jones urged.

Keith was slightly below average height, medium build, brown stubble, pale skin. The canteen was filled with half a thousand similar entities. Blank disks being programmed by essentially the same system that had successfully turned people into psychopaths for thousands of years.

"I don't like cabbage!"

Even now, as they prepared for their first deployment, they didn't feel like killers. They felt like lost children, and that was as it should be. Now, they just needed to accept a new daddy—or, rather, a whole hierarchy of daddies. Eat your cabbage like daddy says, then go and kill the bad man.

"Jesus, Burt, just eat the fucking cabbage or don't. Just stop the fucking whining!" Sten shouted.

Burt, the spotty youth, glowered at Sten, who was sitting a few places away, and sawed through a chunk of rubbery flesh. He speared the chunk of gristle and began chewing. Keith looked at his own plate. He would have liked to have a little tantrum of his own, but he had been here before. The groups had been mixed again, and relationships were still being defined. Keith knew the other 'boys' would latch on to weakness. He remembered that petty mistakes in the first few days would take terms of heroic behaviour to undo.

The afternoon was another briefing. The entire company was seated on flimsy plastic chairs, obviously designed for children—Keith couldn't tell if this was:

a) due to incompetence,
b) the effects of crushed budgets, or
c) devilishly refined psychological priming.

The session kicked off with the Major standing on a podium and giving another long, motivational speech about the importance of their mission. Keith wasn't listening. Instead, he was looking at the vast collection of seized weapons arranged on folding tables, standing neatly about the repurposed mess hall, which was another colossal distended dome of concrete. Soon, people across Europe and Asia would use nasty things like that to try to kill him.

After the speech, the men were instructed to wander around and familiarise themselves with the improvised killing gear on the tables and ask questions of the soldiers, who had made themselves experts in their use and construction.

The first thing Keith looked at was an old tablet, with a bulky case permanently epoxied onto it.

"Custom radio shoe," a red-bearded engineer explained. "Interfaces to the tablet and provides a standard TCP/IP stack implementation. It's a custom radio that does 10km line of site, good wide-band for use in urban environs. Also does Doppler and artificial aperture. This one can sense a beating heart through 80cm of concrete wall. The Chinks or the Clans build these, and they find their way into the hands of everybody from the Surgies to the ZKF."

"What's a usage scenario?" Keith asked, trying out the jargon.

"Battlefield comms and command and control. A bunch of Bohunks with these can run a pretty tight squad. GPS target designation, friend or foe tagging, secure comms. Does pretty much the same as our HUDs, and they can put them together for a thousand times less."

The spook moved on to a squat armoured drone, with four tiny gimballed jet engines and pylons for mounting nasty little weapons.

"With the right software, these things can work as a swarm, spotting and attacking, feeding everything back to their battlespace," he said, nodding back towards the tablet on the previous table.

"So if our enemies are tooled with all this, what's our edge?"

The answer came too quickly and was accompanied by two seconds of unblinking challenge that communicated equal measures of amusement and pity.

"Training and experience."

"Great."

***

A spring morning, replete with shafts of sunlight, babbling brooks and singing birds. On such a morning, Keith allowed himself some optimism.

Training had been exhausting and tiresome—months of helpless frustration at the arbitrary beck and call of pedantic officers—but it was a cake-walk followed by a picnic compared to deployment. His new job mostly consisted of flying around the Balkans, while getting shot at by every diverse ethnic category conceivable. For over a year, their battle-scarred little bunch had been variously inserting themselves between terrorists and critical infrastructure, or genocidal maniacs and their terrified dehumanised victims. On this bright spring morning, Keith's squad was backup to a team of forensic anthropologists investigating rumours of some nasty little local episode of racial intolerance.

Vivid green leaves burst from twigs in a slow-motion explosion of vitality. Life, which had been biding its time waiting for an irrefutable sign that the bleak, desperate winter was over—finally convinced there would be no more cruel tricks to catch naive, irresponsible optimists—was partying with Mardi Gras abandon. The winter had been especially bitter. The evidence still lay skulking in the shadows, hiding from the spring's ascendant sun as it went house to house, banishing the last resistance of the winter; melting solidified cores of snowdrifts into translucent ice sculptures riven with chambers and miniature waterfalls.

In a moment of weakness, with all the rural beauty and the spreading contagious enthusiasm of spring, Keith had found himself thinking pleasant thoughts. It had been a tough few decades for the planet, but there would be a spring. Okay, there had been some erosion of freedom, but fewer people were starving these days. Perhaps it was worth it? In another thousand days, Keith would be out of the army and free to start again. The AIs would continue to take on more of the dangerous, routine and tedious jobs and leave Keith free to focus on living and loving.

It was then, with his visor up, thinking these pleasant thoughts—the warm spring sun on his face—that Keith found the grave. He felt his foot sinking slowly through the thin crust of ice, into something soft below. Looking down at his feet, initially he did not understand what he was seeing. Gigantic teeth seemed to close on his foot, but, as he sank deeper with a crackling popping, teeth resolved to ribs. His armoured foot was dragging grey flesh and skin into the abdomen as it sank, leaving incongruously white bone to catch the morning sunlight.

'How the fuck did I end up here?' he thought to himself.

As he waited for the forensics team to clear him for foot extraction, he let his mind wander, trying to find an adequate answer to the question. He knew the first-order reason: he was here because he had humiliated his boss in front of the smug bastard's entire management team. Perhaps he was getting numb, because, literally knee-deep in horror, Keith still smiled at the pleasant memory of punching Ben in his grinning face.

They were in a field a few hundred metres away from the

small, semi-abandoned village. Semi-, in this case meaning that about 35% of the houses were empty. Most still had roofs, and the amount of growth in the gardens—large bramble bushes, but no trees—suggested they had not been empty long. This fitted with the data in the file. The last time anybody had slept in those houses was March 2028. 65-35 was the ethnic breakdown of this village before the *incident*. Without bringing up the information in the files, Keith couldn't even put names to the factions: Orthodox/Protestant? Or possibly Catholic/Sunni? Maybe Shia/Sikh? No, they were too far West for that. It didn't matter in the end; all rotting flesh stank the same.

Keith shifted his weight slightly and felt something snap. His chunky, articulated knee sank another few centimetres into the rotting hole. Although battlesuits might have initially sounded like a great idea—extra armour to stop you from getting killed, extra strength to help you carry your pack and your extra big guns—after wearing one for thirty months, Keith was very aware of the limitations. They ran out of juice, they always seemed to break down at the most inopportune moments, they were ridiculously loud, and they made you three times as heavy as an unencumbered person—which, in certain situations, could cause you to break through the shallow top soil and sink, knee-deep into the putrefying flesh of carelessly buried villagers.

Then, of course, they were a bugger to clean. Keith knew, if he didn't do a proper job of washing the sticky ichor from his knee joint and pulling the shattered bone fragments from between the hydraulics, the stupid thing would jam, and he would be carrying his oversized pack and unnecessarily large gun by himself.

Once given the all-clear, Keith used a stick and bunches of leaves to wipe from his leg the filth that had once been a person. He was glad of the faceplate's filters. The rest of his squad sat around watching as the forensic techs, in their white disposable paper suits, began the equally unpleasant job of collecting the skulls and personal effects of the victims for cataloguing.

Curtains twitched in still-occupied houses and farmers stopped to watch from a safe distance. In the past, Keith had been tempted to use the excessive firepower his suit gave him to gun down the surviving locals, who were almost certainly the perpetrators of the genocide; but today, he just couldn't summon the energy to care. He knew in the next village the 65% would belong to the other faction and revenge was already taken care of. Or, maybe somewhere, they were taking care of it right now, making sure there was something foul for Keith to smell next spring.

'How the fuck did I end up here?'

For a more satisfying answer, where would he start? He had spent months on this seemingly straightforward question. There was no single linear theme that could be traced from some idyllic past to the present clusterfuck he found himself embroiled within. The difficulty was pruning the branches that had merely exacerbated the situation, honing reality down to just the threads that left masses of today's human population hungry, murderous, or dead, while a much smaller number enjoyed, hyper-concentrated, the remaining wealth and privilege.

He had decided the minimum set of factors should be something like:

> *Too many people.*
> *Too much corruption.*
> *Too much stupidity.*

He liked this set. He had pared it down over the past several months, iteratively removing candidates such as greed or racism, which he realised were mere subsets of Stupidity or Corruption. While this was technically true for 'Too Many People' too, he thought it was such an enormously idiotic error that it deserved its own space. Keith had often been tempted to remove everything but 'stupidity' from his list; but this was too easy. It let off the hook the arseholes who had seen the train coming and who, through either apathy or greed, had failed to lift a finger to avert the wreck.

The rest of the day was spent macabre body-sitting to prevent the perpetrators messing with the site before it could be properly audited. Without a visible deterrent, there was also the danger that villagers would try to murder the auditors and file them, along with the evidence of their past deeds, in the grisly library of flesh.

Keith watched a film on his visor while sitting with his back to the dig. Every few minutes he scanned the scenery, keeping track of the few locals going about their daily chores: gathering firewood, milking cows, ploughing the rich, black soil. Finally, the Head Tech sent an SM to their Platoon Leader, saying they had what they needed, and they all started to pack up their shit. The Techs made no attempt to hide the body-filled gash they had made in the tranquil rural scene. From the air, as they dusted off to head home, it looked like a frozen frame from a zombie film; headless bodies—many still wearing the cheap, nylon clothes they had been murdered in—seemed to be clawing their way out of the ground.

Ample inspiration for another midnight nightmare, another brick loosened from the crumbling ruin that had once been Keith's sanity.

After three hours in the belly of their old, noisy tiltrotor, they arrived back at the squad's current home—a scruffy collection of shipping containers, low concrete buildings, and tents stuck up on a blasted Armenian moor. A foot patrol was returning, and the perimeter was awake, blazing with blue halogen lights that painted electric shadows across the surrounding muddy scrub.

Keith walked the suit to his dorm and then climbed out to let it trot the rest of the way back to its hanger for maintenance and charging. He wanted to go off-base for some maintenance and charging of his own, but tomorrow they were shipping out for a ten-day deployment to Uzbekistan, or somewhere. Surgies were running wild from Tashkent to Ashgabat, causing havoc with the ageing oil infrastructure. If Keith and his chums didn't intervene, the dominoes of globalisation would topple, and it would be another cold, hopeless winter for millions of shivering peons across Western Europe.

A few people tried to chat as he made his way via the shower block and canteen to his bed, but he couldn't see the point. Instead, he climbed straight into his bunk and shook into his palm, what he estimated to be, a non-lethal dose of sleeping tablets. As he slid toward numbness, a simplification to his causal factor list for the world's sorry state shimmied into his tired mind. He metaphorically crossed out the old list:

> ~~Too many people.~~
> ~~Too much corruption.~~
> ~~Too much stupidity.~~

…and replaced it with the more accurate and far more succinct:

> *Such a lot of arseholes.*

```
symbolic transformation:
source: multi.
target: social.carnivore.land.homo.english.uk
style: thesaurus.accurate
--
Tinkerbell.Tursiops [@0809aB772]
Spray.Larus [@nB86249M718]
```

Get down here. I've got your fish.

[I am] jubilant. [I] want my fish. Give [me] my fish!

Do you see my nose?

[I] don't see my fish. Don't eat my fish. Don't eat my fish!

Here is your fish. I'm holding it with my mouth. Dive down to me.

[I] see my fish. Don't eat my fish. Delicious fish. More fish?

Stella can see Spray, the seagull, labouring back up into the stiff breeze, carrying a struggling sliver of silver, half-swallowed and protruding from his beak. Spray might have no concept of 'I', but he has a firm operational understanding of the possessive: 'my'.

'No more fish here. Where are the fish now?' Tinkerbell asks.

'[I] don't know. [I] will fly high,' Spray the seagull replies. The cognitive interfaces do their best to translate species-specific syntax into intermediate semantic maps and back again.

The speck that Spray has become spends minutes circling the floating farm and the surrounding sea. Down below, Tinkerbell is diving into the blackness in case squid or other tasty denizens of the deep happen to be lurking beyond the range of Spray's vision.

A little map pops up, showing the location of Spray's latest tag. Stella wonders, again, how the map must look to Tinkerbell. Chris told her once that the interface is different for each species, and even differs between individuals.

'Fish! Fish there - 30 degrees from the sun, 1300m,' the seagull sends.

The interface learns, acquiring specific eccentricities as program and user grow together. Spray has no concept of a metre, or degree, but Stella's Spex and the hardware in the bird's head work together to translate, back and forth, smoothing out species-specific cognitive idiosyncrasies.

'I have a fish for you here. It is on my head. Do you want to sit on my head?'

'[I am] jubilant. [I have] another fish.'

Stella can't help laughing as she listens to the exchange between her two friends. Spray has such a focused one-track mind that he is funny, until he becomes annoying. Whereas, with Tinkerbell, it is almost like talking to another person—wait, Stella corrects herself—Tinkerbell *is* a person; she must mean it's like talking to another human.

Once in another life, Stella had not known what it was to have a friend. She had not even known friendship when it had waited patiently for her acknowledgement. Her childhood had been an emotional roller coaster, featuring her mother in the lead role, alongside a merry-go-round cast of violently unpredictable cameo parts drawn from the region's generous pool of psychotic talent. The chaos had never left room for reliable interactions or stable relationships. Everything was mixed up: guilt, shame, anger and a deep confusion that had grown outwards from the kernel of her baby mind to become the fractured bundle of irrational loops her teenage self had inherited.

Then her mother had died.

The spindle for the reel of crazy was gone and Stella had unravelled. Another couple of years and the scars would have written themselves so deep that even a lifetime of expensive therapy would have left her brittle and broken. However, just as her bipolar mother had gone—leaving their monopolar family without a nucleus—a cavorting, bickering, fascinating, new family had arrived in the shape of Chris and his menagerie, a distributed, diverse tree of associates and affiliations.

Chris, the kindly beleaguered patriarch, had set up Sagong Marine for Stella after she had rescued him from his sinking boat. He had made her CEO, and Tinkerbell had been employee number one. Initially, at least to Chris, it had been something of a game. Tinkerbell enjoyed playing with Stella, and they would spend time together whenever Chris' work brought them near the Farm. Slowly, the girls had bonded and, one day, Tinkerbell—who had always been very much a free agent—had decided the Farm was her home.

Perhaps recognising something broken, Tinkerbell became Stella's benign older sister; but, over the years, as Stella grew in confidence and ability, the roles slowly reversed.

Although Spray is also technically an employee, he doesn't have the mental capacity to deal with abstractions like money. His finances are managed by Sagong Marine's Sages, Synthetic Cognition algorithms which look out for the seagull under the terms of the UN's REVOBS legislation. Spray will never be more than a much-loved, but infuriatingly naughty, ADHD-addled younger brother.

Since casting her mind and reputation out into the Mesh, Stella has picked up second-degree friends from Chris and Tinkerbell and now has a bunch of spectral cousins, who drift through her world, while simultaneously sharing with her glimpses of their corporeal real lives. They form a soft-family, distributed across the globe: from Belize to Bäna, Kidderminster to Zilistan. In this new accepting social environment, she has managed to unlearn many of her childhood lessons taught by fear and vulnerability.

***

The sea is in one of its friendly moods. The sun sparkles off breeze-ruffled waves, like a million camera flashes from a stadium crowd. Stella sits on the roof of the Admin Block above the Pink Pussycat, watching her friends and listening in on their bickering as Tinkerbell perpetually goads Spray into performing useful work, i.e. finding fish shoals from above, so Tinkerbell can decimate them from below. Tinkerbell always shares, as promised, and Spray always expects to be cheated.

Stella had rushed through her morning chores at the Pussycat, mostly dishwashing and vegetable chopping, and now, responsibilities discharged, she is free to focus the rest of the afternoon on running her marine survey and maintenance operation—or, as Chris would describe it: "Sitting in the sun, dangling her feet into the salty water, and chatting through Spex with her friends."

She hasn't attended school since she started Sagong Marine. She can learn so much more wired into the world, than listening to her teacher's out-of-touch gibberish.

```
[Connection request] Chris [@ChrisTuck3rR] has requested
a Sagong Marine personal channel.
```

"Hi Stella, working I see."

"Not really, my two employees are still on a break… and have been since yesterday afternoon!"

"Oh well, at least they're cheap," Chris sends back. "How is that bloody seagull?"

Advances in Bio and Nano technology have only recently managed to cram the whole package of radios, nanotube neural interfaces, amplifiers, and processors required for Spex-style communication into a package small enough to fit inside the fantastically compact avian braincase. Spray had been rescued—or kidnapped, depending on the perspective—from a rubbish tip by a couple of Osmanian boys Stella had met through her new network of friends. The bird had somehow tangled itself up with a half-swallowed mass of wire, nylon twine, and solidified melted cheese.

According to his original story, the boys, who she knew as Zaki and Segi, had patiently separated bird from refuse and then filled his head with more computing power than a room-full of twentieth-century server racks. The bird had proceeded to become a pest around their great aunt's smallholding; a seagull with attention deficit disorder is hard work. The eighty-year-old woman insisted it was possessed by an evil djinn and waged a constant war on it with broom and shoe, until Stella, while listening to the constant stream of amusing and outrageous anecdotes, had recognised a mutually beneficial situation and offered Spray a place in her company.

The logistics of translating the bird's only tangible assets, i.e. its physical body, across thousands of miles and dozens of tense international borders, had been simplified when Zaki had worked out a way to hack Spray's avian navigation instincts. He had created a few hundred virtual herring gulls and sent them to surround the lone corporeal avian. The oblivious seagull, now embedded within this virtual flock, and reassured by the security of a gigantic ball of screaming pals, had headed off across the Mediterranean and out over Egypt. They had guided him by directing the virtual birds and relying on Spray's innate flocking algorithms to drag him with them; fish factory, to rubbish tip, to abattoir, until, amongst his imaginary friends, Spray had made the last crossing accompanying a Çin sewerage boat destined to dock with the Farm.

Spray had hardly seemed to notice the change in scenery; but, from the little emotional clues the fish-eating machine leaked, he seemed happy with his new role as organic surveillance drone.

Adding Spray to Stella's crew made the Sagong Marine franchise a viable competitor in the search, inspection, and sub-aqua maintenance space. At first, they had only bid on contracts from the Farm, sending—or, rather, politely asking—Tinkerbell to inspect nets or rescue trapped RVs, but as the positive reviews flooded in, they began to get contracts from other vessels and organisations. The company was saving up to get Marcel a new pair of Spex to replace the hand-me-downs from Stella. They also needed to get him a decent set of scuba gear. There was only so much Tinkerbell could manage without hands. Marcel was good underwater, but hampered by his puny human lung capacity.

Stella had tried to recruit more dolphins from New Atlantis, but they were notoriously easy-going and contented and, therefore, difficult to motivate. There was virtually nothing they wanted that the sea and their King didn't already provide. Capturing and chipping any of the few remaining wild dolphins was technically difficult, because they were so rare and justifiably wary of human beings. More importantly, it was against the laws and provisions of the sovereign state of Atlantis and would result in embargo, retraction of visas, and the recall of any Atlantean citizens from the offending entity or organisation.

"What's your job sheet like for the next few days?" Chris asked.

"After the nets, we've got nothing until next Thursday, when I have Tinkerbell scheduled for a yacht wash and wax. The owner is racing from Vancouver to Sydney, and I've told him we can do the job while he is underway."

"Sounds interesting. How's that going to work?"

"Tinks will wear her new gimp mask with the scraper. She is not exactly thrilled, but she'll do it."

"Fine, don't annoy her too much, though, or she might look for a new job!"

"It's all good," said Stella. "She's not going anywhere."

"Okay. Then it sounds like you don't need Spray for that, so that fits well with a new tender I just found for us."

Chris might have set up Sagong Marine for Stella out of charity, but he was not dumb. He kept his equity in the company and was still the second largest shareholder—behind Stella, but ahead of Tinkerbell and Spray. Marcel had never officially signed up, preferring instead to work as an employee—and, to Stella's perpetual ire, preferring to spend any spare income on vintage collectable cards and overpriced flowers to impress his succession of crushes on the Farm's limited population of eligible females.

Stella always welcomed new work for the team.

"Cool, what is it?" she asked.

"Search and Tag," replied Chris. "A ScumWhale was crippled in a storm last week and has gone rogue. They have teams out looking for it, but the GPS is offline, and the thing is not returning comms."

"Maybe it sank."

"Probably not; it was sighted narrowly missing a fishing boat three days ago… here." A map tag arrives. "Anyway, we get a retainer of twenty Coins a day, the finder's fee is two hundred, and there's at least one other operator working on this one, so let's try to deliver on it. Okay?"

"Great, that will go towards some of the new kit we need! I'll see if I can get Zaki or Segi to work on it with their network."

"Right, that would work," said Chris. "Don't go too rich with their cut, though; this is a sweet deal. But it's a good idea; they might have assets overhead that can help."

"What about the GPS tag?" asked Stella. "Where do we pick one up?"

"See if you can swap one for some of your grilled crab or something. They only cost pennies. There is bound to be one somewhere; every net float has one. Get the gypsies to write a macro for Spray. I'll send you the schematics, so they know where to get him to wedge it."

"They call themselves the Kinfolk, not gypsies," she chided. "And anyway, that all sounds a bit complicated for the seagull… He's not super smart, you know."

"If that doesn't work, just get him to perch on the thing until we can locate them both. I've got to go now, Stella. You're not earning enough for me to retire yet, and my two enormous daughters need to eat."

They signed off and Stella noticed Tinkerbell and Spray on their way back to the Farm. Obviously, they couldn't physically fit any more fish into their stomachs and were finally ready to do some work. She pinged Marcel to tell him to get ready, then sent a mail with the new job to Zaki and Segi, offering them a couple of Coins to run a search through any botnets and compromised satellites they had access to.

***

Stella's Spex chime musically, *@5eggE* has come online.

[Connection request] @5eggE is requesting to join your room.

"Hey, Stella, how's it going?"

"Hi, Segi."

"What ya doing?"

"Working. Did you get my mail?"

"Yeah. I saw it come in and called. It shouldn't be a problem. Want to help me do drone escorting for a delivery?"

"No thanks, I'm with Tinks and Spray. They've just finished eating, which took all morning!" Stella sends an exasperation emoti. "They are going to help me fix some rips in the pen nets."

"You spend too much time with lower lifeforms," Segi sends back, accompanied by a moping trollified self-portrait.

"I'm lucky to have a job. Anyway, how about you! I couldn't get you or your brother at all last week."

"Yeah, lots going on. We've got a new Spirulina bioreactor online, and I needed to set up an incubator for a new project. So what's the job? If I can save up a bit of Coin, I might come and visit. It sucks being stuck here!"

"You should try being a penniless uneducated orphan for a while if you want to see what sucking means! I've been there and done that!"

"Yeah, but at least you never had to actually suck anything!"

And, with that, Segi signs off before Stella can ream him. It's true, though; she's lucky, luckier than her mum had been. It will soon be five years since her mother died, and Stella, who will be twenty in a few months, knows too well the career advancement options for an orphan teenager living on a floating brothel. She knows that not all the girls on the Farm will be lucky enough to land a job as CEO of an international corporation.

The Madam had taken her aside a few of years earlier and asked about her plans, mentioning in passing that several of the ship captains had been asking. *Because she was very fond of Stella, in case she was ever interested, she could set up an auction and would give her a good cut of the proceeds…*

Stella had told her she was very grateful for the kind offer, but her company was starting to make money and, if things continued to improve, she might not have to work as a whore at all. The Madam, usually as inscrutable as the wizened zen master she resembled, looked sceptical for a few seconds and then showed a rare flash of emotion and struck Stella quite hard on the shoulder.

"Good for you, girl!" she had said, before shuffling off in a flounce of robes and ribbons to greet a group of raucous sailors coming through the swinging doors.

Stella gets a short update mail from Siegfried and notices Spray flap off, presumably to start his task. She rides shotgun in his mind for a while, looking through his eyes while he soars off and away from the Farm. From his internal point of view, the seagull is again part of a reassuring confusion of wings and cries—which, by Segi's careful design, will fly the optimum search grid centred on the most likely location of the ScumWhale.

Once she is confident Siegfried knows what he is doing, she clambers back down from the roof of the Admin Block and heads towards the steps, where Marcel should be getting ready. Rounding the corner, she catches sight of him pulling up his wetsuit. She can't help noticing he is not a scrawny little runt anymore; then again, she is no longer the scruffiest kid on the Farm, either. She has become an enigma, with her posh clothes and the designer Spex that rarely leave her face. She watches him, while he ties his long, sun-flecked brown hair into a ponytail, then pulls the end back through the elastic loop so he has a tight nub of hair sticking off the back of his head. Marcel's grin is the same, though, and he turns and flashes it at Stella before diving off the outer, curving rim into the Pacific.

Tinkerbell is already there and, with a rapid sequence of thrashing oscillations, swims off through the water to meet him. Stella dips into the dolphin's stream of perception and watches as they play for a few minutes, until Marcel has to come up for air. She stops the remote viewing when she realises she is intruding, a feeling that makes her inexplicably jealous.

"Hey, Stella, look at this!" Marcel shouts, then dives below the waves again.

Before he has swum down more than a metre or so, Tinkerbell places her nose against the soles of his bare feet and pushes; torpedo and propeller, they go straight down. Marcel has one hand on his nose and is constantly equalising the pressure in his ears as they dive quickly to twenty metres. Then, they pause their descent, and Marcel glides over the dolphin's back and places his mouth over her blowhole. A burst of bubbles slows to a trickle as Marcel breathes the air Tinkerbell is exhaling. Then it's back to the torpedo position, and they drop another thirty metres.

"We don't need that SCUBA gear!" Marcel sends.

Stella doesn't know quite how to reply.

Another day, another dull, dangerous deployment. Just 183 scratches left to make on the wall of the cave in his mind.

Keith got up, ate breakfast, grunted the required obscenities to his comrades, pulled on the new set of techno underwear that had miraculously appeared in his locker, and finally zipped himself into the suit's removable, pressurised onesie. As he walked to the hangar, the clean fabric felt luxurious against his skin; soft silk quilting over Kevlar, seamless and gel-filled at the joints to avoid pressure sores. The sensory deprivation they all suffered from the command structure's autistic communication hierarchy meant any vague trace of information was sucked dry and chewed over for relevant content. So, the arrival of new underwear, a rare and portentous event, was interpreted as: 'You will be in constant combat for the next two weeks with no time to change your kaks.'

The front of Keith's suit was splayed open, ready to envelop him as he stepped backwards into its cold grip. Once his heels were hard up against the back of the metal feet, the shin armour hinged closed around his calves. He repeated the process with chest, arms and head, leaning back and letting the exoskeleton's segments close around him until it enveloped his whole body, like an articulated ski boot. The head-up display showed the fuel cells were at 99% capacity—two days of normal activity—and all systems were showing green. To the left and right of him, more young men were being ingested. When they were all suited up, the Staff Sergeant hustled them out across the pitted tarmac and onto the knackered tiltrotor they knew so well.

It didn't turn out to be two weeks of combat; the production of the latest adrenalin-soaked montage of hurt to be burnt into Keith's psyche had barely lasted four days:

Drop off — yomp through the night — close on a group of tents — massacre at Surgie training camp — IED — ambush — "Medic! Man down!" — pinned down by mortars — fuel cells low — snipers in the night — bullet through the foot — "Useless fucking suits!" — "Where's the fucking backup?" — "We're on our own." — big push back — grenades — big gun — bayonets — blood...

The squaddie let go of the Bohunk's legs. They were barely kicking anymore; more like twitching. Keith let the knife slip from his bloody fingers. The gritty floor was covered in pools of frothy red broth. They were inside the low walls of what was probably the ruin of an ancient, one-room house, although it might just as easily have been a goat pen built at any time over the past five thousand years. To get to the ruin, the two had just spent six hours carefully crawling a five-hundred-metre circle from their last position, where most of the rest of the squad were still hiding. Once there, they had quietly slid over the back wall and killed the sniper lying behind a pile of collapsed stones that had once been the front wall. Ignorant of the danger, he had been peering intently through his scope and patiently pinging rounds down towards the exhausted, petrified squad below. He hadn't noticed them. He probably thought they would still be clunking around in their stupid suits and hadn't expected two silent mammals to come slinking out of the night to cut his throat.

They had made as little noise as possible; and, if they were lucky, the other nest across the valley wouldn't have noticed their arrival. Keith rolled the body out of the way and lay down on his chest in the pool of warm blood. He checked his GPS and pointed the dead terrorist's dependable Russ rifle towards the second sniper position. Through the sights, he could just make out two men: one lying on his stomach, the other sitting with his back to the wall, smoking a cigarette.

Keith's buddy took up position next to him. He had unslung his own rifle and was also looking across the valley. With its superior sights, it would be no trouble putting a bullet into either of the enemy soldiers.

"I'll take the smoker," Keith said, selecting the less critical target.

Keith counted in a whisper and, on three, they both squeezed their triggers. The sniper's body spasmed as the high-velocity round entered his chest. Keith wasn't so lucky with his shot. The bullet went over his target's head, smacking into the wall and peppering the flinching soldier with slivers of stone. Before Keith had a chance to line up a second shot, he felt a recoil next to him and watched through his scope as the smoker spun round and slumped down to the floor. The minor shrapnel lacerations on his face now the least of his worries.

That took care of the little group of Bohunks that had been harassing them for the past two days. A couple of the survivors had tried to make a break, but without sniper cover to keep Keith's squad's heads down, they were easily picked off as they ran, their warm bodies making easy targets in the cold night.

Keith's squad was in a bad way. Most of their suits were out of juice and little more than scrap. Their macho, oversized weapons were impossible to carry unassisted. Four of sixteen were dead—including the squad leader. Another three were wounded, including Keith, whose foot had a hole through it. Bandages and boot held on three toes that were only connected by a flimsy mess of skin and flesh. Keith hopped and slid back down the side of the valley to their temporary base, where, with impeccable timing, word came through that they should expect backup and Evac within the next two hours. Nobody had the energy to bitch that, if command had bothered to tell them about the relief a bit earlier, they wouldn't have needed to risk their lives in a midnight raid on the sniper nests.

While the adrenalin ebbed, sick and trembling, numb with resignation, they waited for the thrum of propellers that would announce the arrival of their ride.

They had started the night's operation in icy-pitch black-ness; but, while they were waiting, the sun had inched its way up a quarter of the featureless blue dome, and it was becoming uncomfortably hot for those lying on the hard, ochre clay. Thousands of years of winter storms had washed out a deep channel in the pebbly clay, which snaked between large rocky projections sticking up like colossal termite mounds. The slopes of the valley were dotted with olive trees and low shrubs. Semi-feral goats ambled amongst the boulders and bushes, cropping the few blades of grass left over from the previous winter's rains.

The squad had set up in a curve of the gully, sheltered by its steep outer bank. Keith had started worming his way up the hill at 2 am and hadn't got more than an hour or so of sleep before that. Additionally, for the last three nights, he had been intermittently shot at and blown up, while trying to sleep inside a humming suit of power armour—humming, in the sense that the fuel cells, hydraulics, and environment control systems were incessantly noisy, but also because it stank to high heaven of sweat and piss.

He was tired. They all were. They lay like a herd of elephant seals; the two functioning battlesuits were the colossal males, Keith and the rest were the diminutive females, nestling in amongst them for protection. Backup and Evac were coming. They didn't have to march to the next engagement or dig in for combat, so they were grateful for this opportunity just to lie and wait.

Their tiltrotor, familiar from its engine's painful, irregular whine, came into view around the end of the valley. A small herd of goats broke in a frenzied dash across the scrub, as the droning harmony of the propellers became the roar of a thousand paddles slapping bare arses. It flew overhead, then banked and circled once before coming back to hover a hundred metres to the south.

Like reluctant school kids dragged from sleep by their alarm clocks, the squad grumbled to its feet. It was 10:45. The tiltrotor sank towards the ground, shifting impossible amounts of dust into the air, with its blades slicing the red soup in their fully horizontal configuration. Partly obscured by the throat-clenching dust, Keith watched as four suited figures dropped on lines from the rear ramp, presumably intending to set up a perimeter.

As the roaring, dusty chaos approached, a cackle of surprised yelps from the waiting soldiers indicated something unexpected was happening. Keith grabbed his helmet and used the HUD to zoom in on the four dangling men, now flailing wildly as they descended. Their heads were whipping from side to side like toddlers having a tantrum, while their limbs were bent in what looked like unnatural and very painful directions. It was grotesque, like a cybernetically enhanced epileptic fit. There was a blast of automatic weapons fire, which seemed to come from within the plane, and a neat row of holes appeared in the side of its fuselage.

"Fuck," shouted Keith. "We're under attack!"

To his left, there was a nasty gristly sound, followed by a terrible scream. Both armoured marines in working suits seemed to have contracted the same fitting disease. The scream had been from an unarmoured squaddie, who had been punched in the nose by a fifteen-horsepower fist. Keith assumed the guy inside the suit would probably be screaming too, unless he was already dead. His armoured hand had grabbed onto the chin of his helmet and was wrenching his head from side to side at neck-snapping speed.

While Keith had been looking away, one of the tiltrotor's engines had caught fire. It was sliding sideways at an appalling angle, with one wing practically scouring ruts in the earth, while dragging the four spasming battlesuits through the brush. Keith watched in horror and, a second later, it was over. With a wallop of a concussion, the plane became an expanding sphere of shrapnel, immediately obscured by a mini mushroom cloud of fire and black smoke.

It was impossible to get close enough to the thrashing suits to help their buddies. They were both almost certainly dead anyway, as were the former occupants of burning wreckage that only two minutes ago had been their ride home—or, if not home, at least to somewhere slightly less deadly than this region bordering the Levant, which the Caliphate reluctantly recognised as Zilistan, but which many locals still referred to as Osmaniye.

The wind changed direction, suddenly pressing down the thick, black smoke to envelop the pathetic group of human wreckage that was Keith's squad. With colossal effort, Keith got onto his knees and pressed his face to the floor, trying to find a pocket of clean air to breathe, but there was no chance. He began to hear peals of ragged coughing and vomiting around him as his colleagues were forced to breathe in the toxic air. He crawled as far as he could and, despite viciously slicing his nose on a piece of red hot plane debris, managed to keep his jaws clamped shut. Finally, with his diaphragm clenching uncontrollably, he gave in and took a breath. He began to cough immediately; with each wracking intake of breath, the acrid burning pain grew worse, until his vision filled with glittering points of light and he blacked out.

Her illusions had tarnished since leaving Prussia. Most had faded on a single night with the dying echoes of a gunshot. Ayşe rarely recalled that nightmare. She and the boys never discussed it, choosing instead to remember Anosh as the life-loving, irrepressible optimist he had been.

Both boys reminded Ayşe of him in their own ways. Sometimes, she would sit under the shade of a tree, shelling pistachios or knitting, and watch them working; they were industrious, like he had been, and always had an infinite stream of ideas to be realised.

Ayşe never blamed herself, but only because she actively blamed the killers who had taken the boys' father from them. She might not torture herself, but she knew she had been wrong to leave without him. Looking back, she could recognise she had been, at least partially, out of her mind with fear and anger, searching for some way to escape the violence and danger that had surrounded them. She had seized on the simple messages broadcast from the re-energised Caliphate; beguiled by its promises of dignity and safety.

Although many promises had turned out to be empty, as she watched Prussia and the rest of Europe lose their souls to the machine, she still believed that, under other circumstances, coming here would have been the right choice.

The world was turning into something unrecognisable. Ayşe didn't understand the big picture; she never had, didn't try to. It had been the same when they were young. Anosh would try to explain things, getting super animated and overthinking everything, while she had relied on her instincts and the unwavering moral code her parents had baked into her as a girl.

Faceless was how she managed to describe it—inhuman and faceless. On the rare occasions she had used Spex to meet with her old friends in Prussia, she felt as though she was visiting a zoo, watching animals with glassy eyes following routines so ingrained that they had worn ruts into their minds.

At least here she felt there was continuity with the past. The Caliphate's enthusiastic revival of ancient traditions seemed to meld well with the local superstitions and simple way of life. People seemed content, happy to ignore the swirling change around them and let themselves be nurtured by the same abundant landscape that had sustained their ancestors for millennia. They were unusually content, not addled with angst or stuffed full of superfluous, unquenchable needs. Ayşe suspected the Caliphate's metaphysical firewalls, and the population's own poverty, insulated them from the whispering voices that urged so many to consume their way relentlessly towards unrealistic self-destructive aspirations that would always remain an eternal shimmering mirage on the horizon.

There was violence. They lived in a region controlled by the Zilish Workers Party, the ZKF, and occasionally there was trouble with ZKF road blocks or things blowing up. But Aal's husband had been a Zil, supporting the cause, and out of respect they were mostly unaffected by the fighting. Aal was Ayşe's mother's younger sister, a barely remembered figure from childhood holidays. She was an *interesting* old woman, with a fearsome local reputation as a reader of coffee grounds and significant pronouncer of fates. The awe and fear she commanded was another positive factor on local relations.

Today, Zaki and Segi were digging soil for some new horticultural enterprise. They both had their shirts off: Segi was broad-shouldered and tanned, while Zaki was smaller and paler, his body contorted by the old injuries that had twisted his spine and cramped his arm. His eyes and spirit were bright, though and, at least in his own mind, he was the head of the family now, having taken on the burden that night, when he alone had seen his father's body, a jerking puppet, dangling beneath a departing helicopter.

Their work was at the edge of a small lake they had created a few years ago, by damming a creek that ran through Aal's land. Winter rains filled the basin, which slowly dried out once the rains stopped, but kept the soil moist enough to grow plants that would not usually survive the blistering furnace of summer.

Zaki straightened his back and grimaced, his damaged vertebrae and ligaments popping in protest.

It had been a few weeks since the last rain, and the water level was just starting to drop. It was early May, so there was a chance of more rain before summer got going, but now was the last chance to transplant the heavily gene-modified bamboo seedlings they had been nurturing in the barn's incubators over the winter.

***

A decade ago, constrained by increasingly claustrophobic

corporate nannying, libertarian hackers had begun their work on an egalitarian alternative internet. Its manifesto, of equality amongst Bits, would be coded into its lowest protocol layers. The Mesh—as they had called it—started out as a nerdy hobby, a subversive platform for avoiding censorship crossed with an urban techy art project. It had caught on quickly amongst the ethical hacktivist community taking a stand against the Man. Then, as the national firewalls had risen, it had grown, spreading its mycelia through the fabric of a tattered, exhausted society; offering nostalgic amusement, proudly shared and curated by people who hoarded old media from a time before entertainment became saturated with grinning, enthusiastic propaganda and laced through with malignant hate.

In the earliest days, its exponential growth had been easy to miss; then, it crossed a critical threshold, becoming a pandemic of exuberant liberation racing between mushy minds and spreading secondary infections into mounds of formerly obsolete repurposed hardware

Its creators, seeing the unexpected scale of this success, realised it could be a template for something truly new. The Mesh was the first, but it was only the vanguard; an exemplar for the ecosystem of autonomous corporations that would follow. The Mesh slowly morphed into a web of self-contained virtual corporate entities, each bootstrapping its build-out by purchasing timeshare slices of runtime on hardware rented with their self-issued Crypto Coins. They justified their existence by offering useful services, and created value for their balkanised currencies by requiring payment in their own Coins.

Owners of hardware hosting a FAC, a Fully Autonomous

Corporation, would receive rent, paid in the relevant Coin, for all the clock-cycles, bandwidth and storage used.

The FAC's decentralised, self-organising model, was immediately seized upon as a way to evade stifling censorship and to design and manufacture all the kit, drugs and guns—which a frustrated technical underclass believed were not only a basic human right, but the legitimate technological inheritance of every curious tinker.

Having evolved well past its initial information transmission function, the Mesh was a platform for hosting and discovering every conceivable form of embargoed technology sourced from an ever-growing menagerie of FACs.

Using commodity components found in superabundance across the world's supply chains—only adding specialist or 3D-printed parts when absolutely necessary—most Mesh-sourced designs could be manufactured in any basic low-tech workshop. For micro-controllers, processors and exotic ingredients too difficult to manufacture locally, or too easy for governments to control, the network would provide. GliderKiteFAC became the switched packet network of matter. A physical extension to the Mesh, its fleet of elegant, soaring global wanderers could deliver small quantities of anything to almost anywhere. Their onboard intelligence and real-time knowledge of the planet's weather—sourced from other Mesh-hosted FACs specialising in meteorology—allowed the high-altitude gliders to efficiently use wind and sun as their power. They were not fast—it might take weeks to soar from one side of the world to the other—but they were cheap and easy to manufacture. Segi and Zaki used them to deliver the graphene porridge they produced in their long, snaking bioreactor tubes and to bring in new trinkets, like MeshNodes, BugNet controllers and other specialist parts they were not able to fab themselves.

The majority of FAC initiatives focused on drugs or weapons; however, as the approach matured, more ambitious designs began showing up with loftier aspirations.

By the twenty-first century, the number of dangerous objects that could be strapped to a rocket had become seemingly limitless. Governments, paranoid of losing their monopoly on weapons of mass destruction, endeavoured to maintain an iron grip on the rocket science of booster technology. This obviously infuriated the nerds for whom space was almost—if not actually—a religion. 'Open Launch Vehicle', or OLVFAC, was one of the Mesh's most ambitious children. A multi-stage entity, it had ICO'd with significant funding in an initial research and engineering aspect. A complicated system of rewards and pay-outs had bound together an unlikely coalition of Kinfolk, hobbyists, and retired ESSA engineers to work towards the FAC's goals. These early contributors had been paid in its basically still worthless Coin, with the optimistic expectation that, if successful, their rewards would increase in value as the services OLVFAC planned to offer began to look less like late-night fanboy fantasies.

After years of slow gestation, OLVFAC had surprised not only its haters, but also many contributors, when it delivered a design for a beta-test that hadn't simply exploded on the launch pad or spiralled erratically into the sky to be euthanised.

A few weeks after the first test had successfully lifted off from its secret location, a chorus of furious denouncements for reckless irresponsibility had followed a second launch—which had soared into low Earth orbit and delivered a cargo of frozen pizzas to the impoverished, insubordinate, but ravenously grateful crew of the ESSA space station.

As the Mesh had exploded with hysterical delight, calmer minds had realised this was more than a silly prank—it was yet another sign that Pandora's box wasn't yet empty.

***

The sun was almost overhead and Ayşe was heading back. Zaki watched his mother walking slowly towards the house. She was carrying a bundle of spring onions and salad leaves in a small, wicker basket. He thought she looked aristocratic, with her erect posture and measured stride. Segi was nearly finished planting his own bundle of thin bamboo stems. Zaki took the watering can and soaked the roots.

In a few years' time, the genetically modified plants would grow into a good-sized clump. Once they really hit their stride, the new canes that emerged would grow to reach five metres high and twenty centimetres in diameter. Hopefully, if conditions were right, amongst the giant bamboo stalks, a few monster mega-canes, over a metre across at the base and fifteen metres tall, would stab out of the ground.

Thousands of iterations had been built in simulations before the first OLV test rocket had left the pad. The ingenious design, concentrating all the value in the reusable engines, meant the rest, the bulk of the rocket, was basically a long stiff tube that could be built of almost anything.

One day, the massive bamboo stems, thin-walled cylinders,

would become biologically derived fuel tanks. OLV rocket and aviation modules would be attached to the thick, woody rhizome at their base of the mega-canes. The engines would chug fuel from *nanosilk* balloons stuffed inside the bamboo cylinder. A flight computer inside the aviation module would compensate for most physical deviations away from perfect aerodynamics. And, even when things went wrong—shoddy workmanship, badly distributed weight, or misaligned payload—the computer would notice, ideally after only a couple of seconds of flight; then, if the planned launch was not feasible, the whole stack would gently land again, with a full report of changes to be made before trying again.

Life on Aal's farm revolved around the old lady's routines and habits. Although sometimes frustrating or baffling, it provided a welcome stability to Ayşe and her family. On a typical day, they would eat chicken or lentil soup in the courtyard. Other women from the village might join for dinner and, once the teenagers had helped clean away the dishes, the visitors would ask Aal to let her inner eye range over grains of coffee that held the answers to this life and the next. The boys would roll their eyes dramatically at this unscientific nonsense, while grudgingly getting on with whatever ad hoc chores their great aunt or mother had found them. Finally, responsibilities discharged, the brothers could get back to whatever building project or online campaign they had put aside while RL forced its fleshy needs to intrude.

The Çiftlik house had stood for three hundred years, the centre of the local community from where the Agha had run the estates. Sometime towards the end of the twentieth century, it had gotten a telephone and, shortly thereafter, electricity. Thick bundles of old telephone and electric cables still draped from its corners, tangled and useless, hanging like prolapsed organs.

For the family, the first couple of years in their new home had been a time of constant adjustment. The landscape and habitations that had passed outside the dusty windows on their drive east were universally rustic, but there had been no tent cities or mysterious military musterings, no decaying piles of rubble or terrifying herds of half-feral children throwing stones, while exhausted mothers looked on with catatonic stares. Instead, there was a yellow fuzz of dry grass with olive and pistachio trees dotting the landscape. Wherever a valley held the promise of running water, clusters of plastic tunnels appeared filled with tomatoes and squashes.

The lizard and mice personas within, looking out, felt that, for the first time in a decade, it might be possible to survive here, without the risk of having to eat one's own family. The vermin's approval conferred peace.

For the first weeks, Zaki had been silent and unresponsive. Ayşe and Siegfried had tried to talk, but attempts at cheery reminiscence inevitably ended with misery, anger and sobbing.

Aal had welcomed them to her home with tears and fetishistic ticks. They had received strange henna runes on their hands and blue glass eyes for the ends of their beds. Segi feared great aunt Aal, who dripped molten lead into water to banish evil and lit candles or burnt bunches of herbs, filling the house with thick yellow smoke and exotic smells.

Even Zaki, who thought himself an atheist, reductionist warrior, admitted to feeling a little freaked out by this muttering mound of black cloth, dreading her bony hugs and terrifyingly hairy upper lip.

Somehow, though, the superstitious rituals helped—washing away painful reality, replacing it with mystic patterns. She embodied the occult, as if inside the layers of fabric, wrapped in an infinity of gold chains, there was something numinous wandering the old farm.

Their mother brushed off such comments: Aal had always been 'gifted', always found lost money or charmed stubborn warts.

The boys tried to keep out of the old woman's way. Anything she didn't understand was considered a waste of time, and so she was always finding them tedious, dirty jobs that took precious time away from their growing graph of friends and projects.

The old buildings were arranged in an L-shape. At the corner was the original ancient sandstone house. To its left, was a tatty concrete box with white paint flaking off its metal windows, and iron rods projecting from its corners. The third building was a vast ancient barn, more recently reinforced with concrete and roofed with corrugated metal. Inside, an old tractor slumbered under a thick residuum of chicken shit. The boys had begged and, with their mother's support, had been given the space to make their own. Here, they fled the looping maelstrom of cleaning and prayer.

Geographically, they were close to Eden and the cradle of civilisation. Unlike most of the storm-lashed, nutrient-leached Earth, they had food and water in abundance, but the most advanced form of power generation technology within five kilometres was the hybrid motor in their old Land Voyager. In second place came the self-sustaining exothermic oxidisation of cellulose.

A few months after they had arrived, they had been sitting and watching sticks burning in an old iron range.

"History is going backwards," Zaki observed.

"How so?"

"It's like science and technology is receding. It's ignorance and superstitious bullshit out there."

"You mean the Caliph?" Segi asked.

"Yeah. Of course. He's turned the clock back to 600AD. But not just them; it's the world. People are forgetting how everything works."

"That's just here. It is weird, though, but it's not everywhere."

"You might be right," said Zaki. "I wouldn't even know. *Scheisse*! How could I know? I need to drive to town to get online! This is so backwards!"

They had been experimenting with methods of smoking the hemp that grew wild around Aal's farm. It had tasted awful and made them cough, but they recognised its effect as they tried, with difficulty, to estimate the rate of technological contraction based upon observations. It seemed to be about two years/km/year. They were about five kilometres from the nearest town and, in the decade since the great backwardation, the farm seemed to have slipped a hundred years into the past, losing TV, telephone, and the automobile along the way.

They had resolved then to stop the trend, at least locally, and be the grain of dust around which a crystal of competence could grow. They would hold back the erosion of human progress. They knew their father would have approved. It gave them purpose, helped them get through those first difficult months. Years later, it would continue to define who they were.

***

[Connection request] @5eggE, Stella Sagong [@SagongMarine] is requesting to visit.

"Hey Stella, what's up?"

"Hi Segi. Nothing much, just thought I would drop by to say hi." Stella looks around the cluttered lab, where her subjective presence has materialised. "What are you doing?"

"Working. We are printing out some new [garble] designs…" Segi turns away suddenly, his lips moving indistinctly, obviously talking to someone that the privacy filter is blocking Stella from seeing. Some seconds pass; Segi's face becomes blurred. Stella wonders what emotions are now being edited away, too.

[Connection request] @2@k1, Zaki has requested to create a room from this conversation.

Stella blinks an affirmative and, as the privacy walls fall away, Zaki materialises standing next to a bench—which, as it resolves from behind the blur, acquires the bodies of several partially dissected frogs and a gruesome collection of bloody implements. Zaki looks like something out of a Gothic horror—blood-streaked, wearing a stained lab coat, with his bent back and twisted clenched hand.

As the audio kicks in, Stella catches the end of Segi's tirade of brotherly abuse.

"Hi Stella," Zaki says, smiling weakly. "Nothing personal, but this is supposed to be classified. Kin eyes only."

"Oh right," says Stella. "Yeah, no problem. I just dropped in for a chat really. I can come back another time."

"No, don't! Zaki's just being a dick." Segi gives his brother another evil look and peels off a pair of bloody gloves, which he drops into a recycle can. "Let's go outside, where there are not so many arseholes."

Zaki shrugs and delves back into the rat cranium. Tiny dead paws shiver.

Siegfried guides Stella towards the zip-lock door in one wall of the plastic, 'clean room' tent the boys have hung from the beams of their great aunt's barn. Leaving the white and chrome of the tent, they are seemingly transported a hundred years back into an Arcadian agricultural vignette.

They emerge into the sunshine of late afternoon. Across the dusty ochre yard, alternate rows of orange and pomegranate trees step off towards the low hills in front of them. To the right, a track cuts through the scrub of low, hairy plants interspersed with olive and bay trees. It leads down into a shallow valley and, eventually, to a town whose name Stella has forgotten and can't be bothered to look up.

Segi sets off the other way, through an arid garden of towering sunflowers and chilli plants potted in big old square tins. The faded yellow and red labels are incomprehensible to Stella. Rampant, neurotic chickens scratch in the dust, flapping and panicking at Segi's unsettling proximity as they walk towards the house. The chirps of crickets and cicadas saturate the air.

Stella's Spex have been playing tricks on her sense of direction, subtly twisting the virtual world to give her as much perceived space as possible, but now, they warn her she is getting close to the edge. Allowing the reality of the Farm to bleed through and intrude on her perception, they show the perimeter. If she keeps walking, she will topple into the sea. Focusing on the ghostly reality that has become visible, she turns around and faces back towards the Pussycat to give herself more room to walk. Then, ignoring a brief flash of dizziness, she spins the virtual world—barn, Segi and surrounding countryside—around herself with a gesture and is, again, facing in the same direction as Segi. He is waiting as she sorts out the geometry at the intersection between her two worlds.

She follows Siegfried through an ornate pointed arch in an ancient wall of clay bricks and weathered, pale stone. The wall separates the house's courtyard from the estate's outbuildings. An ineffectual wooden door—a honeycomb of termite-excavated sawdust—hangs off gnarled hinges.

Its ornate antique carvings preserved by layers of flaking, pale blue paint. The wrecked old door is wedged open by clumps of weeds that have grown through its cracked wood.

The ownership of the sprawling Çiftlik house is complex. According to the ancient, but still relevant, Ottoman legal system, it belongs to the descendants of the old Agha—Stella had looked it up, apparently a type of Ottoman lord. In a parallel legal world, after a series of literally Byzantine legal transformations in the 1940s, it had been granted to their great uncle, the cook, who had stayed on and kept it from utter decay during that turbulent time. Every few years, somebody would arrive from Constantinople or Medina, carrying a briefcase full of yellowing documents covered with fabulous signals and flamboyant looping script, in possession of a firm belief that the land belonged to them or their clients. They were usually invited in for tea, politely listened to and then, once a suitably impressive posse of local armed men could be assembled, unceremoniously run off the grounds.

Inside the wall is another world. A large, low fountain tinkles in the centre of a courtyard, split into beds of lush vegetation by paths of marble slabs. The immediate impression is grand, but at a second glance it is all appallingly chaotic and dishevelled; the awnings of pantiles and black-stained oak look like they are ready to collapse any century now. Rotted wooden pagodas and benches protrude from the green chaos like the spars of sunken ships, and the mix of plants seems determined more by a process of unintentional artificial selection, favouring the varieties that can tolerate intermittent but radical pruning, than any intelligent horticultural design.

To Stella, coming from a floating aquatic doughnut with extreme population pressure and no soil, it might as well be Eden. There is not a lot of green on the Farm. Oranges and lemons are a precious luxury. Here, they hang surreally from the trees like pixel glitches.

"Segi, this is beautiful!"

The boy looks around, as if taking it in for the first time, then shrugs.

"Yeah, I guess. It needs looking after, though. Mother is always saying they should re-plant the garden, but Granny won't let her touch it. I like the avocados." He gestures towards a big tree at one corner.

"No, it's all magical. I wish I could smell all the flowers!"

"Umm, I was going to go through to the dining room, but we can sit here for a while if you like."

He leads her around an old fig tree to a stone bench that faces across one of the paths to the broken, shimmering surface of the fountain. Two small frogs, disturbed by their arrival, plop into the water. A cluster of wasps and hornets lift briefly from the gloop of fallen exploded figs that slather the bench. Segi sweeps the lot off with a dried palm leaf and sits down. Stella hesitates, not wanting to:

a) *get covered in sticky fig, or*
b) *get stung by a giant wasp*

—but then she remembers, she is not really there.

They talk about random stuff. Stella is happy to have somebody beyond the horizon of her floating enclosure to gossip with. The Spex pull back a veil and she can no longer consider the Pussycat's whores or the Farm's serf children her equals. Even Marcel has changed, she tells Segi, relating the morning's demonstration of extreme interspecies tandem freediving.

"Are you saying he kissed her blowhole?" says Segi.

"I'm not sure that kiss is quite right," replies Stella. "But I guess that's what it looked like."

"Weird!"

"Right!?"

They pause as they watch a bent bundle of black cloths and scarves emerge from the murky cave of the house's great doorway. An old woman approaches, carrying a copper tray with a jug and glass of some milky liquid. She says something in Osmanian, which Stella hears through layers of translation as:

"Talking to ghosts again, are you!"

"Yes, Granny, this is Stella."

Segi gestures to what, for the old lady, must appear to be an empty bench.

"Pleased to meet you," the woman says in Osmanian, not quite looking in the correct direction. "Would you like a drink? It's my own lemonade."

"Granny, she can't drink!"

"Well, at least, it's polite to ask!" the woman mutters before heading back into the house.

"So that's your great aunt? She seems nice," says Stella.

"She is; she doesn't quite get it though, offering you a drink! She really does think you are a ghost, you know."

"I am sure she doesn't. She was just being friendly."

"No, she does. Me and Zaki have explained dozens of times how the Spex work—how they create a virtual geometry and surface it with textures captured from our cameras—but she can't get it. She knows what a ghost is, so she stays with that. I don't argue anymore."

"Maybe it doesn't matter. When you think about it, what's the difference?"

"One is technology," replies Segi, "the other is the crazy superstition of an 85-year-old lady!"

"But, in either case, you are still sitting alone on a bench, talking to a disembodied spirit."

"Yeah, I guess…"

"We can't touch each other, not even if we wanted to…"

It's not that he would necessarily be averse to touching Stella, but he feels the floor of the conversation is slipping away. He rallies and changes the subject before he is forced to examine this thorny philosophical area in any more detail.

"How's Spray getting along?"

Stella looks at Segi for a couple of heartbeats, very aware he has changed the subject, then replies, slightly coolly,

"He's part of the team now."

"Good! He was a pain in the ass. Like I said, for Granny, technology really is black magic. She was convinced he was possessed by an evil djinn."

"Yeah, I know. It worked out well. We're pretty lucky to have him around."

"How's the search for the ScumWhale going? Any leads?"

"No, but we'll find it."

"Sure."

"Right, well, I guess I better get back to work then," Stella says.

"Really? Okay then, me too, I guess."

They say goodbye. Stella drops back to the blistering light and broad blue horizons of the Farm, feeling even more irrationally irate than before.

'I am a bloody ghost between worlds,' she thinks. 'Even a

dolphin gets more human contact than I do.'

Back in the reality she left, Siegfried shrugs at Stella's sudden departure and heads back to the lab to see how Zaki is getting on.

***

The boys are *Kin*. They belong to a virtual clan of hacktivist, tinker nerds. They are nodes in a vast, mostly illicit, peer-to-peer economy of reputation and Coin. To their youthful, unjaded minds, it was incontrovertible that all wrongs must be righted and everything broken fixed. There were no shades of grey. It is only with middle age that an appreciation for the inertia of stupidity arrives, an understanding of the appalling effort involved in changing even the smallest silliness; hence, corporations—made up of a monoculture of plump, middle-aged, men—are rarely idealistic.

The Mesh was the libertarian answer to a broken, compromised internet. It was illegal in most of the world because corporations didn't like the change and the lack of control it represented. They could have tried to adapt their business models to it—some might even have prospered—but that would have meant risk and effort. It was far easier to nobble a few of the current-batch politicians and bribe them to sponsor a crackdown and extend the status quo. In the FWDs (the Former Western Democracies), it was common to find shuffling gangs of clean-up squads—bands of the poverty-wracked unemployed and petty criminals, herded by bored police heavies in riot armour, using long, waving wands, like the antennae of injured ants, to pick up tell-tale radio chirps from concealed MeshNodes; locating and smashing the offending devices and, with each expunction, earning a few more calories in food tokens.

The Mesh was vital. It was the trunk and branches upon which the vast, complex ecosystem of the digital counter-culture grew. Those with seditious aspirations, but only a minimum of relevant skills, could earn their stripes with entry-level work by expanding its network and filling in its holes. Despite governments' best efforts, the trend was inexorably towards growth. All over the world, eager hands were busy printing, wiring up, and scattering its nodes. The Mesh automatically rewarded its employees with Coins, calculating priorities based upon the locations of bottlenecks and black spots, and adjusting pay-out to demand and congestion.

Unlike the FWDs, although the Caliph rejected the evils of anything more complicated than a windmill, his government concerned itself more with sanitising spiritual dogma than with smashing plastic gadgets. The Caliph didn't care which sinful network his marketing department used to send out propaganda.

Confident in this continued ambivalence, the two brothers had set out to create a bubble of twenty-first century by saturating the surrounding countryside with solar-powered MeshNodes. Their success in bringing bandwidth to this data desert had sped them through the lower ranks of their chosen clan; moving them quickly from Script Bunny, through Luser & Lamer, before finally propelling them to the *lofty heights* of Noob. Over the last couple of years, Team Silicium had continued to provide 'missions' to match their expanding capabilities. Spray, the seagull, had helped them unlock the cybernetic bio-engineering badge, but it was a gruesome business and earlier experiments had ended badly for a stray cat and a hedgehog. After eventual success with Spray, appalled at all the blood and shrieking, the young journeyman Kinfolk had refused to deal with mammals and birds anymore. Even amphibians were a test to their stomachs. Luckily, Silicium's latest delivery for beta testing had been a batch of BugNet nodes designed to target the arthropod nervous system instead.

"Anything?"

"Static… wait, I've got the carrier… no, still just the carrier."

"The chip should have grown in by now."

"Maybe it's different in a locust."

"Hey, here is something."

The sinusoidal trace, like a neon worm on the oscilloscope screen, had sprouted hairs. Zaki hopped off the bench, where the unfortunate locust was taped—naked filamentous wires sticking out of its head—and bent over the device. Siegfried played with the controls, until he had zoomed in on the crest of one of the waves. Under magnification, the hairy spikes showed themselves to be curved stepped crenulations.

"Try to send something."

Siegfried moved to a Companion lying on the bench next to the oscilloscope and fiddled with the screen, until it showed a basic schoolbook diagram of a locust. He touched the wings. The locust on the bench struggled, legs and body twitching.

"Cool! It's working. Run the training data—wait, the camera is not set up properly."

Zaki took the old webcam and angled it out on its makeshift desklamp boom until it was pointing directly at the locust. Then, he brushed off the white sheet of paper, laid out under the insect, and Siegfried hit the big calibrate button that was pulsing green on the Companion's screen. The locust started twitching again, and a progress bar started inching across the top of the screen. The kids watched for five minutes as the twitching became more localised and controlled. The tablet estimated another two hours to go before the locust's responses to the chip's signals were fully mapped.

The tiny chip, one of a batch of ten the boys had recently been delivered, had 6400 pits on its surface, each containing an artificial neural stem cell. When the chip found itself in the right environment, the engineered stem cells would grow out of their pits and form synapses with the host nervous system. Once grown, the device, the size of a grain of salt, would turn its insect host into a mobile MeshNode. In addition to all the normal Mesh functions, a user in possession of the right digital certificates would have access, via an encrypted radio interface, into the locust nervous system, allowing, amongst other things, for it to be remotely controlled like an organic drone.

The two boys high-fived, then headed back to the house to scrounge up some food, while they waited for the locust to finish its spasming.

"What was that *Schatz*?" Ayşe asked, looking up from her book.

"I didn't hear anything," Siegfried replied. He was standing at the sink washing potatoes. Ayşe stood still, listening.

This time, they all heard it, a sound like distant thunder that rattled the glass in the windows. Without a word, Zaki jumped up and headed upstairs.

"What's going on?" Ayşe shouted.

"No idea, Mum. Better get Granny inside, though."

Up on the roof, Zaki scanned the horizon with a big pair of antique binoculars held awkwardly in his twisted hand. He had completed one circuit of the flat roof and was starting a second, when he saw a big mound of black smoke showing behind the hills to the east. He looked down at his tablet screen; it was at least eight kilometres away. Quickly fitting the tablet's camera into an adapter, he screwed it to the binoculars and took a poorly cropped picture of smoke looming behind scrubby hills. He labelled it with his best guess location and a timestamp, then dropped the image into the house's tactical awareness system.

Zaki assumed it was either an accident or an attack on the nearby pipeline by the Zilish Workers Party. The area had been calm for a while, but a neighbour recently lost three animals when a stray munition landed in his goat pen.

Segi stood at the kitchen counter with a collection of

Companions arranged in front of him. The ancient, wooden shutters of the house had been pulled closed and secured. It was dark; shafts of sunlight forced their way through cracks in the wood and gaps under doors. Segi's face was lit from below by the screens. Having made their life within the borders of a fundamentalist religious state that was locked in conflict with domestic and foreign actors, attack and conflict were known to be non-zero possibilities, and the boys were prepared.

The house was running the latest version of the Team Silicium Command and Control package. Segi himself was a minor contributor and had sent in bug reports and small patches over the past couple of years. The map showed a red blob roughly located at the explosion, which had been triangulated from microphones on the roof. A few kilometres away was Zaki's dropped pin, with its annotated photograph attached. Both pins probably represented the same location, and their separation simply error, but Segi left them as two separate pins until more intel arrived.

Another marker, yellow this time, indicating unknown or neutral actors, dropped while he was watching. It was uploaded by somebody called "ASALA86". Siegfried tapped the new pin and flicked the details to one of the Companions. An obviously pre-prepared message appeared and played: a group of men, their faces hidden by keffiyehs, stood decorated like Christmas trees with assorted weaponry. One of them spoke to the camera in Osmanian, taking credit for a "decisive victory" against the forces of occupation. Segi fast-forwarded to the end of the sequence to see if there was anything else tacked onto the end; there wasn't.

Zaki thundered back down from the roof and out of the

side door.

"I'm going to see if our insect is ready," he shouted, moving with the half-skipping shuffle he used when he wanted to shift quickly.

The locust had stopped its fitting. Now, driven by the computer in its thorax, it was flexing each leg in turn, slowly extending and retracting its limbs and mandibles with very un-insect-like deliberation.

A few minutes later, while Siegfried was watching, two more green markers appeared, one after the other. Unlike the other pins, these were moving. One stayed close to the house, metadata showing it climbing up five hundred metres. The other was cruising away at a smooth ten km/h on its way towards the distant event markers. Segi selected the video icon on the first of the new green pins. Once the ascending drone was high enough to make a direct line of sight to the source of the explosion, he zoomed in and was able to resolve a blackened crater filled with wreckage. A huge cloud of smoke was still rising from it.

The second pin represented the cyborg locust. Its video showed a highly pixelated vista flowing by, anything over ten metres away a vague blur.

***

The ground and the backs of his hands are bright red. They seem to be soaked with blood. He begins coughing and vomiting and blacks out again.

He tries to open his eyes, but they are stuck shut. He touches them with his hands and, in the darkness, tries to wipe away some of the sticky shit that is everywhere. When he begins coughing again, it feels like he will never stop. Each time a cough breaks out of his chest, it feels like an elephant is kicking him in the side of the head.

He might have blacked out again for a few seconds, but at least this time there is some continuity. He fumbles around on his belt and pulls off his water bottle, lifting it to his mouth and taking a long swig. The water makes him realise how bad his mouth tastes. He takes another small gulp and swirls it around his teeth and throat with his tongue and spits the phlegmy cocktail onto the dirt; more coughing. When the lights stop flashing inside his skull, he cups his hand and tries to pour a little water into the well of his palm. Focusing on his left eye, he wets the matted filth and, eventually, manages to blink the eye open.

When the dazzling glare subsides, he realises he is sitting just over the crest of a small hump of rock and sand, surrounded by blood and vomit, presumably his. About twenty metres away, his squad is lying motionless in the gully. He had only been their commander for a day, following the unfortunate death of their old sergeant. The smoke has thinned out and is now blowing the other way, leaving enough untainted air for him to breathe again. He shakes the water container, trying to judge what is more important at this point—binocular vision or rehydration. His screaming headache decides for him, and he gulps down the rest of the bottle. He then attempts to get to his feet; however, when he puts any pressure on his left leg, a massive wave of pain crashes into his mind, annihilating all sense of self. He had forgotten that he had been shot through the foot; looking down at the source of the pain, he can also see that his boot seems to be melted and his trouser leg charred.

The next time he comes around, he checks his watch to see how long he was out. The scratched piece of plastic on his wrist is lifeless, either from the eWar fallout that downed the tiltrotor and turned the suits into murderous traitors, or from concussion and general physical abuse. Looking instead to the sky, the sun seems to have moved at least a hand's width since the attack. Using a miscellaneous piece of wrecked aircraft as a crutch, he hauls himself up onto his good leg and begins to make his way, as quickly as possible, back over the ridge to check for survivors—and, incidentally, loot the unfortunate corpses for any water and drugs.

He had managed to check the mauled burnt cadavers of three of his squad, when he catches the distant drone of a petrol engine; it sounds like a motor bike.

"Fuck!"

He breaks into a comical shambling, adrenalin now the only ally against the appalling pain and the beckoning maw of unconsciousness. He needs water. It is hot and dry. He has been bleeding and vomiting and will certainly be dead within a day without it. So he takes precious time locating his pack and some bottles from the belts of two of his former squad. Then, he hobbles away from the engine sound as fast as his ruined body will carry him.

Collapsing behind another small hill, close enough to hear the cackling merriment of the gloaters when they arrive, his tenuous luck holds; nobody climbs the hill.

He must have passed out again, or possibly just decided to have a little sleep, perhaps even given up entirely and chosen to die—if so, at least he had the sense to die under a tree. It is late afternoon and, somehow, he is still not dead. He rubs his functioning eye, which had been stubbornly trying to glue itself shut again, and scans the landscape. A thin ribbon of smoke is still rising from the crashed tiltrotor hidden behind the crest of his little hill.

He edges around the tree, putting its bulk between him and the crash site. Then, he notices the biggest grasshopper he has ever seen. It is sitting on a branch and seems to be watching him. As soon as he makes eye contact with it, the big green and red insect lifts a front leg and, with slow elegance, seems to beckon him forward. Then it turns and jumps away a few metres before deliberately shuffling around to look at him again. He watches the insect tip its head from side to side, its big triangular eyes looking directly into his own. It hops away once more; then, in three big jumps, retraces its route, perching on the same branch where it started out. It does this three times before bouncing off for five jumps or about ten metres. It climbs up a dry stalk and begins pointedly staring at him again.

The man knows he is tired and probably delusional, but even if he is hallucinating, perhaps this is the mechanism his subconscious mind has chosen to motivate him to move again. Shrugging, he picks up his water bottles and blunders off into a sea of agony, following his totem spirit insect.

For ninety-seven years, the legal firm Baphmet, Halibut & Joyce had provided for London's most discerning clients with discreet services pertaining to bruised reputations. Protecting clients from unsympathetic attention, they had become experts at constraining the press and finessing public opinion.

In the 1990s, when George Baphmet had taken the helm from his father, he had made his mark by steering the firm from law into marketing. Despite being something of a fuddy-duddy, even then, George had recognised the promises of technology. Less a visionary and more a stickler, he had nevertheless pushed his firm to apply data-driven techniques to divining the fickle fads of public opinion. Technology advanced, and algorithmic marketing became real time and indistinguishable from advertising. BHJ moved with the times.

Three decades later, storms of financial chaos had raged with such abandon that, looking back, pecuniary archaeologists would identify an economic extinction event. Despite being in his seventies, Old George had continued to steer the firm with a steady hand. When demand from the private sector slumped, he moved BHJ into consulting government spin masters. Seeing the writing on the wall for the consumer, grasping an opportunity unseen by his many competitors, who were themselves capsizing and drowning on the turbulent financial seas around them, George had pivoted BHJ once again. The mothballed server rooms, full of decommissioned marketing bots and 'Synthetic General Intelligence' racks, were rebooted and repurposed from peddling products to pushing ideas. BHJ had joined—or possibly created—the computational propaganda market. As the firm grew exponentially for the next decade, Old George, now nearly ninety, had never looked back.

***

The pattern was relentless: a click, followed by an irregular rattling whirring that went on for minutes. It put the mind on edge. It was like listening to a voice while phlegm catches erratically on its words; wincing at each warble, wishing for a cough to clear the congestion.

No noise made it in from the city outside. For a soulless, hermetically isolated hotel room, it was incongruously cold and draughty. Erratic gusts from the air conditioning fluttered the curtains, letting the neon colours from the city's visual insanity seep through. Footsteps and voices from the corridor broke the silence or joined the whirring backing track.

Ben was willing himself to sleep, but each click or happy chuckle from returning guests in the hotel corridor was seized by his jet-lagged brain as an excuse to rev up back to full wakefulness. It was late. As the hours ticked by, the chance that he would not sleep at all increased, raising the stakes and throttling up his anxiety.

He looked over at his Spex lying on the table by the bed, set to show the time, two sans serif numerals shining out of each lens. He stared mindlessly at the faintly glowing symbols. It was 3.03 am. The last number flipped to a four, then a five...

Something on the bedside table moved suddenly and he

started. In a panic, he called for illumination. The room's lights came on in time for him to see little spiky legs scuttle across the surface of the table and out of sight. A few moments later, he saw them again, scooting across the hotel room floor.

"This in Benjamin Baphmet, room 4182. There's a cockroach in my room."

"Oh, so sorry to hear that, Sir!" said a female voice. "We can move you immediately."

"It's three in the morning. I don't want to get up in the middle of the night and move bloody rooms."

"I understand. I can send up a boy with some spray..."

"Are you a human?" Ben asked impatiently.

"Yes, Sir, I am. Is there anything else I can do for you, Sir?"

"Really? You don't sound it."

"Yes, Sir, really. I am Hualing."

"Okay then, Hualing, please pass along the message to your supervisor that I will not stay in a hotel that is infested with insects. I will check out tomorrow."

"I am really sorry to hear that, Sir, but I will pass on the message to my manager."

"Yeah, well then, I will try to get back to sleep! You are shitting on my day here, Hualing. Do you realise that?"

"Sorry, Sir..."

Ben hung up before he could hear the remainder of Hualing's sincere-sounding apology.

***

He probably managed to get some sleep between four and six, but it was difficult to tell. Eventually, a gentle clicking from his Spex terminated limbo, and he got up out of bed, showered and got dressed.

His auto was just pulling up through the feather gate as he stepped out into the multi-storey atrium. The gate's fronds parted to let the vehicle through, sealing again behind it. He hadn't checked out. He couldn't be bothered. He guessed all the hotels in Shanghai would have cockroaches, anyway. Ben didn't like the city much, but it was not an opinion grounded in specifics. It was more a default racist position, emergent from a privileged traditional upbringing and an inherent superiority complex. He would admit that it was cleaner and worked better than European cities—the feather gate, designed to keep out polluted air, was more habit than necessity now—but he was a product of the old school, and his institutionalised cultural narcissism wouldn't let him acknowledge that Çin was booming.

Corrupt, centralised totalitarian regimes had proven to be the most competitive at the game of eco-apocalypse. The world had spiralled down towards a financial black hole, but Çin's centralised power structures had enabled the country to skirt the event horizon. Ben knew only a little of the brutal measures the population had endured. Farmers had crops confiscated, first-tier cities suffered terrible rationing, and areas deemed non-strategic or politically uncooperative were left to fend for themselves. Elites and strategic human resources were relocated. Refugees were shot. Millions starved. But the ruthless application of *herd before individual* nationalism had allowed the country to slingshot out the other side of the Great Global Contraction and it was, once again, the powerhouse of the world's economy.

The Forwards had tried to adopt the model, but were too squeamish to make the tough calls. Instead of balls-out violent oppression, they opted for media-delivered pacification and token-provided welfare.

Ben got in and the car slid into traffic. They stayed above ground for a few hundred metres, shuffling intricately, until their auto had found, and magnetically joined with, a few other vehicles going in the same direction. Then, all the autos, arranged as a single mini-train, disappeared into one of the narrow, single-lane tunnels. While the car flashed along underground towards BHJ's office, Ben checked his messages and caught up on his feeds. Avicons and emoti slid across his eyes, while a soothing feminine voice spoke through his earbuds.

#License Extension @A3_Afaf:
Ben ḥażrat, I humbly report to you that with the assistance of Allāh and solṭān-e banī ādam, we are making strong progress. The WTO decision to uphold the Mosquito's right to express their heirloom genome allows us full autonomy to negotiate the terms with New Jersey and New Orleans. May it please Allāh Exalted that the high incidence of Malaria and Dengue in the bordering jurisdictions provides us with a dominant negotiation platform for establishing a no-bite agreement. I fully anticipate a successful resolution and your role or that of your colleagues should not be overlooked. Proclaim

the glad tidings to your father.
May all the lives of your family be prolonged.
Adil Afif Al-Afaf

#FRIEND_SPOTTER_FILTER>@keith.wilson_9
#OurBoysDown
@TheBritNewsPaper:
Sixteen British soldiers were killed when ZKF terrorists attacked a military transport in a disputed area
of Eastern Osmaniye yesterday. One injured soldier was
reported captured and another identified as Keith Wilson
[@keith.wilson_9] is still missing.

The attack came amid demands of increased ZKF autonomy,
with strong rejections coming from both the Caliphate
and the Osmanian Empire. There has recently been an
eruption of violence across the area. A...

Ben had only been paying partial attention, but when
his Spex tagged a mention of his former employee and
old school chum's name, his eyes flicked back into focus,
and he scrolled back up to re-read the article. Keith was
missing, presumed dead—the stupid arse. However, despite
his instinctive reaction to glibly hate on Keith's assumed
incompetence, Ben felt a fleeting unfamiliar pang of loss.

A faint, dull noise, too refined to call a clunk, indicated
the cars in front and behind had detached. Out of the back
windscreen, Ben watched the lights of the vehicle recede
gently. A soft acceleration and a change in the geometry
of the lights streaming by outside indicated his car had
drifted into a side tunnel.

He was angry and tired. He didn't like travelling out to
the branch offices. He had once enjoyed it; he had loved
lording it over provincial BHJ peons, but even this simple
pleasure had lost its charm. Also, he suffered from the

growing realisation that Shanghai had grown well past the point where it could be considered a minor franchise. Shaun, his one-time assistant and old school victim, now ran BHJ's fastest-growing region.

The market for brainwashing software in Çin had remained protected until recently. Compliant media and Astroturfed grass roots nationalism, in combination with shock and awe domestic oppression, had served the state well, limiting appetite for more modern methods. More recently, though, a prolonged and heroic effort at high-level courting from BHJ had thawed the ice somewhat. Through Shaun's expert supervision, the package of analysis modules and media avatars had been finessed and localised, ready to woo Wu and his committee. The presentations at a series of *workshops*, arranged and sponsored by BHJ at some of London's most luxurious locations, had been a runaway success with the people who mattered in the Party. Some of the inscrutable octogenarians had even chortled and nodded approvingly at the punch lines suggested by BHJ's Virtual Media Sages.

Fucking Shaun had hit a home run!

The car slowed, the forward inertia counteracted perfectly by the rising incline. The tunnel lights changed from a blur to a succession of flashes; they emerged and merged with the surface vehicles, elegantly matching the reduced speeds of the above ground traffic in a ballet of kinetic mechanics. Had he been drinking, there would have been barely a ripple in his glass. At this thought, his hand was already reaching for the cabinet, but the sun blasting through the haze and the tinted windows reminded him it was only eight-thirty in the morning.

It wasn't raining, so Ben let the car drop him outside the building rather than plunging them into the basement carpark. BHJ had the thirty-second and thirty-fourth floors of the sixty-storey building, barely a poplar in a skyline of redwoods.

Ben resented being made to wait outside his father's office. Shaun was inside with an important delegation of officials. Although Ben had arrived only fifteen minutes late, a good performance he had judged, the meeting had already started. He had been about to open the door and barge into the inner office, but the receptionist—polite, pretty, and pig-headed—had refused to be persuaded and had blocked the door and then shown him to one of the deep, leather seats.

When he was offered a drink, he asked for green tea, despite hating it. While he was waiting, he did more reading about Keith and his unit. It sounded bloody awful; again, he felt a pang of empathy and, even more inexplicably, the taste of jealousy.

The door opened and Shaun stepped out. He glanced at Ben—not a trace of emotion showing on his face—then back to the smiling cluster of Çin government officials who were emerging. Ben's father was last out. He looked over at Ben and, seeing him, shook his head almost imperceptibly. As a gesture, it barely registered, but conveyed a megaton payload of disappointment. Shaun introduced Ben, referring to both his corporate title and familial relationship to BHJ's CEO. A big round of smiling, bowing, and handshaking ensued. One of the officials noticed Ben's pink MinxyMouse socks and laughed, making some remark that was left untranslated, but set off a smattering of tittering. Ben's Spex claimed not to have understood, so he just smiled and joined in the laughter.

Shaun excused himself and led the group to the elevator. More smiling and bowing while the door closed.

George turned his back and stalked into his office, turning his head a fraction to check Ben was following.

"What the hell is wrong with you boy?" The door had barely shut.

"What? Being a bit late for a meeting? Fifteen minutes? Come on, Dad, it's not the end of the world!"

"The end of the world was years ago, and it made us a lot of money!" George had raised his voice, recapturing a trace of the destructive force it had carried when he was a young man. Now he was forced to cough. It was a dry hacking which went on far too long before, red in the face, with watering eyes, he finally dislodged the mucal irritant.

His body's weakness seemed to annoy him further. He sat behind the large desk, recovering, resting his elbows on its dark wood and resting his dappled forehead on his translucent fingers. With his bulging, veined head, Ben was struck by how his father looked simultaneously astonishingly old, but also foetal. George looked up with his cold, ancient eyes.

"The stakes are higher this time. Do you get any of what is going on out there, lad?" he said, waving vaguely at the door.

"Life? Recovery?" Ben tried.

"War." His father stared at him until Ben had to look away. His eyes escaped through the window, off over the glass towers projecting into the low-hanging, orange-tainted morning haze. "It's war. Us against them. Do you know who *us* is, or shall I spell that out, too?"

"The company, BHJ, the shareholders, right?" replied Ben. "It's a safe bet you don't mean me, your family!"

"I mean us, the Haves!"

"Oh, Christ, that is crass, even for you, Papi," Ben said, feigning a childish voice.

"Ben, you need to finally understand this stuff. Look at your stupid socks!"

Ben did. MinxyMouse, in blue, against a cornflower-pink background. They had been a present from an ex, before she became an ex. Perhaps, they were a little too Dress Down Friday/Office Christmas Party for an important government meeting.

"Sit down!" shouted George. "I feel like I am explaining the birds and the bees again."

"I must have missed the first time," replied Ben, "because all I remember of the birds and the bees was my biology teacher running out of the class in tears."

"Shut up, Ben!" The older man smacked his flat palm down onto the table with a colossal clap. Ben was genuinely shocked; his father so rarely lost his cool.

George had stood to shout, and now abruptly sat down again, breathing heavily. "My God, if your grandfather was here!"

Ben noted the pulsing vein at his father's temple and the tremor in his hands.

Eventually he continued. "He would never have had a conversation like this with me. You are right, this *is* crass. Such things should be implied. We grew up knowing the terms of our privilege. But I admit it is different now; all the subtlety is gone. Everything blatant. I can concede it's partly the Sages. They can't seem to cope with ambiguity. But you should be able to. You are a Baphmet, so here goes…"

Ben quietly sat in one of the chairs facing his father. He was only partly following the words, too preoccupied by the old man's sunken face and mottled skin to pay full attention.

"First, it's not fair. There is no such thing. Second, there is no way to opt out. Third, you may take what you can." George paused, waiting for something from his son. "That's it. So what follows?"

"Yeah, I get it. You make deals. You make sure you belong to the stronger team, and you try to win. Beat the competition. Win the deals."

"Yes, but why, Ben?"

"To get the biggest pile of money?"

"But a fool and his money are soon parted."

"Are you calling me a fool?"

"A fool is only the dumbest person in the room. Today, you were a fool. Or would have been, if you'd even made it into the room! It's relative. Take Shaun; he was your assistant once, wasn't he? And now, he's my most successful VP. All because he is smarter than you."

"Oh shit, that is cold. Why are you rubbing my face in that now?" Ben said, focusing on his father's face again.

"Because he is smarter than you; he is better at his job. If you are not careful, he will take your—as you so crudely put it—large pile of money."

"Are you threatening me or something? You're going to disown me and give fucking Shaun my inheritance?"

"What do you think? Should I?"

"No."

"Why?"

"Because I am your son."

"Right." The old man stopped and held Ben's indignant gaze. "That's not very fair to Shaun, though, is it? I bet he is not entirely thrilled knowing he's ten times smarter than you, but will never get my Mayfair mansion or a yacht in Monaco."

"Yeah, poor sap." Ben chuckled, relieved he wasn't getting

cut out of the will after all.

"But he will suck it up," continued George. "There is no other way. Everything is stressed to breaking, and everything and everywhere already belongs to someone. Even the things that will exist have been sold dozens of times before they even get produced. Look at that rock. Still billions of miles away up in space and people are already trading its metals. Stand still for a second and someone hungrier and smarter will take everything you have put to the side."

"Dad, I know this. Maybe you were too wrapped up in Shaun's stellar rise, but I have done my share of kicking arse and pulling in deals."

"I know; you were always good at sales. But that's not enough anymore. Intelligence is now a commodity we sell in bulk, not on the golf course or in upmarket restaurants. This is the game changer. Our Sages are intelligence by yard of server rack. That's why Çin is so chummy, because of the control our Sages offer."

"Yeah, and I do get that," said Ben, using his infomercial voice. "That's what we do. We sell Sages and Avatars to governments to help their citizens make the right choices."

"Exactly, and the next generation we have waiting, once we persuade our slanty-eyed friends to ignore the UN and change their laws, will make all people into fools. You control *these* AIs, you control the people."

"But you just said that's us, right? We control the Sages. I don't get it. If it's war, who is the enemy?"

"Haven't you been listening? The crowds of hackers, the Mesh, the Clans, FAC, stupid Niato and his fairy-tale Atlantis. All those idiots out there, building their out of control anarchist internet! The damn *Have Nots*, Ben!"

It was quite an admission.

"I don't think Niato counts as a have not, Dad."

"Might as bloody well be. Anyway, he's worse. A damn class traitor standing with the rest of them. There will always be poor people, Ben."

"That's," said Ben, making quote signs with his fingers, "*King* Niato's point, though, isn't it? There doesn't have to be. That's why they call it luxury communism."

"Christ! You believe that clap-trap? They just want to take what we have and share it out amongst all their long-haired friends."

Ben managed not to roll his eyes. "Okay. I will try harder. I get it. Look, I know I joke around, Dad, but I see what the stakes are. Maybe one day, I'll find a nice girl..."

"Stop it," George said, interrupting. "I am not your mother. Let's finish this off. I have another meeting in ten minutes. Last piece of your lesson for today. This is the final new deal, because the Sages will run everything soon; whoever sets up the system sets the terms. This is the war I am talking about, and believe me, there will be a war, and we are going to win it. The only thing that matters now is making sure that, when this all works through, we end up with our rightful share."

"The biggest slice."

"Unless you want a smaller one? I am sure Shaun would appreciate a piece of yours."

The son watched his father remove a handkerchief from an inner pocket and wipe away a chunky fleck of pink, marbled phlegm that the earlier violent hacking had ejaculated onto the desk's dark green leather blotter.

"No, you are right, Dad," Ben said. "I get it now."

Stella didn't know why she woke. Something, some noise, but now it was gone—no, there it was again. The thump of the coilgun firing and then a thin whine as it recharged.

Who was harvesting in the middle of the night?

The sea was calm and the tool of piscine execution, normally almost silent, was incongruously loud in the stillness. It kept spitting its slugs into the water and, with each arrhythmic slap, Stella became increasingly annoyed, despairing of ever getting back to sleep.

A new sound, a massive cackle of automatic weapons fire, dispelled thoughts of sleep. Adrenalin squirting into her bloodstream washed away any trace of grogginess. She tried to get a status update from her Spex, but the local network seemed to be down; they were flashing an RF interference error.

"Shit," she said quietly as she pulled on her clothes.

Then the screaming started, women and children. There was another loud crack, and one thread of screaming was silent. Stella hardly dared to move. However, the feed drum was not bulletproof, and she didn't want to get hit by any stray fire, so she untied the lid as quietly as she could and pushed her head out to scan the scene. It was quiet again, and dark, almost too dark to see anything, but her Spex helped. The Farm was devoid of its usual eclectic collection of lights, except for the Admin Block and the harvest platform with the coilgun, which were spot-lit by a cluster of insanely powerful beams coming from somewhere out to sea.

More noise: two crouching figures had opened fire from the roof of the canteen. The two sprayed bullets wildly, but were focusing their attention towards the harvesting platform, where Stella picked out at least two invaders huddling for cover by the coilgun. One seemed to go down. Stella might have seen his head explode into a dark cloud before his body sagged over. He was close enough for her to hear the metallic rattle as his gun skittered away across the checker plate. A few seconds later, while the two defenders where still firing, there was an appalling noise and the canteen building began to disintegrate, one chunk at a time. The sound of defending fire seemed to stop immediately, or possibly it had just been drowned out by the minigun, or whatever was shooting from beyond the blinding lights. The firestorm was tearing the canteen apart, walls sagging like some time-lapse shot of rusting metal.

After a few more seconds, the uproar ceased, and Stella was left staring in horror at the destruction. There was no more movement from the sagging roof. There was no more resistance. Either the Farm's militia were dead, or—and more likely—they had decided they didn't stand a chance against the superior firepower and were lying low.

With the resistance crushed, the pirates—for that was clearly what they were—soon manned the coilgun, and the tuna harvesting resumed. They were plainly professionals. They sent the ROVs down to bring back carcasses for loading onto their boat. For three hours Stella, huddling inside her plastic pod, tried to assemble a picture of the action taking place outside by concentrating on the whine of the charging coilgun and the fizz and slap of its discharge.

Eventually, the carnage stopped. The boat was full, or perhaps a rapidly approaching dawn had imposed its deadline on the nocturnal poaching activities.

Stella dared to peer through a gap between her pod and its lid door. The pirates were returning to their tender. The last load of fish presumably already delivered to its freezers. It would soon be over. Luckily, there hadn't been any more violence and she hoped none of her friends had been hurt. She watched as the pirates sat in the launch. But they didn't leave. They were talking, arguing even, pointing towards the Pink Pussycat. Stella's stomach began to clench and, even before she consciously realised what was going on, her heart began to pound.

Most of the men had left the boat again and were walking towards the club—the same building where Stella's aerial home clung. She watched them through her Spex, zooming in, transfixed by their grim faces. Before they got halfway, Stella heard the familiar sound of the club's double doors as they flew open. There was a succession of blasts from a handgun, six or seven rounds in quick succession. One of the three who had left the boat fell, spun around by a shot to his shoulder. The others flew to cover, crouching behind a water barrel and returning fire. Stella saw one fire off two deliberate rounds. There was a surprised grunt and the sound of a body falling to the deck. One of the pirates, who had stayed in the launch, sprinted up to his fallen comrade and began to rip open his shirt. From her vantage point, halfway around the side of the club, Stella could not see who had burst through the doors, neither could she see the results of the return fire. But, from the thin wailing coming up from within the club, she guessed someone had tried to be heroic and was now lying in a pool of blood.

The wailing took on a desperate edge as the men forced their way in. There was a scream and another shot, then crying and sounds she wished she could choose not to hear. After a time, this second brutal harvest was finished. Stella saw the pirates emerge, marching a line of girls in front of them at gunpoint: Stella's friends, barefoot, wearing their night things, shuffling, silent. By now, the sky was orange with dawn and, in the ruddy light, the bloody footprints the girls left seemed to glow.

What happened next was unclear. Perhaps she cried, or made some other noise, but suddenly the men were pointing up at her feed-bin home. Soon, they were laughing and putting playful bullets through its walls. Stella was terrified. She had never been shot at before and was amazed at the violence with which the bullets arrived. Each time one hit, blasting holes only centimetres away from her head, the whole structure vibrated painfully. Something stung her arm, and she was suddenly covered in blood. More bullets slammed into the blue plastic, and she found herself on autopilot, deafened and terrified, wriggling out of the door and tumbling the four metres down to the deck. Before she was even fully conscious again, she was grabbed by the hair and, half-dragged, half-scrabbling, made her way with the others to the launch. The girls were roughly pushed in, falling or crouching for balance, as the little boat rolled with each new arrival.

Not bothering with their dead, the pirates started off without hesitation towards the blinding light. When the boat was about ten metres from the Farm, a figure came running from the huts. He levelled a gun at the boat, and there was a crack. Stella caught a glint from the spear as it left the gun and heard the splash as it bit into the waves, not far away. The pirates found this hilarious. One stood, pulling his trousers down and presenting his bare arse as a target. With another rush of dread, Stella recognised the shape as Marcel and watched, with horror, as he fitted another spear into his gun. The boat was even further away now, so he aimed high, going for range, tipping the gun at nearly forty-five degrees and shot another spear. This time, there was no glint; however, a second later, accompanied by a small grunt, a pencil-thin metal rod materialised, sticking out of the thigh of the already injured pirate.

His friends found this impossibly funny, and even the wounded man laughed hysterically at his plight. Stella suspected they might have helped themselves to the contents of the Madam's medicine cabinet.

They laughed as they drew their guns and then laughed as they shot bullets into Marcel's body. They continued to laugh as he collapsed. They laughed and shot until either Stella passed out or the bundle of his body became too small a target for the joke to continue.

Stella would remember blinding light, then only darkness. Even during the rare times she was allowed above decks, blinking painfully into daylight, there was only darkness.

***

Kids are tough. That might be enough, Chris allowed himself to hope. If he could get to her in time, she might be okay. He had arrived by chopper into the middle of a media circus. He had cadged a lift out from Naha, with a news crew come to feast on the tasty morsels of teenage whores, kidnapped girls, wounded heroes, pirates, and exotic locations. Even now, the world's media would be spinning their plight into dramas and Telenovelas for the catnip they needed to titillate the billions of restless, thrill-seeking voyeurs under their charge.

Chris loathed it. As Stella's boss, and the closest thing she had to a legal guardian, he had already been approached by two separate studios about the film rights. He had wanted to punch the smarmy, grinning cunts in the face, but he knew Stella and Marcel might, one day, need the money to put their lives back together. Assuming either of them survived.

Chris sat by Marcel's bed and watched the boy's chest rising and falling in time with the respirator's concertina. He had once lain in the same bed himself, with Stella and Marcel sitting by him, chattering away.

A Nipponese frigate had been the first to arrive and had rushed the unconscious boy to their sick bay. They had plugged his leaks and poured blood into him until he was fit enough to operate on. Seven stressful hours of delicate surgery were needed to remove the bullets from his torso. The last was lodged in his sternum, having travelled through a lung to get there. The doctors and their Sages didn't know if he had suffered brain damage; his heart had stopped at least once before they could get him stabilised and onto a respirator. After three days, he was moved to the sick bay of the Farm, one of the few buildings that had survived the pirates' raid intact.

The world was divided into three groups: those glued to the real-time feeds and touching back story segments, those who had never heard of Sagong Marine, and a far smaller group of people actively working to find the girls and bring the pirates to various interpretations of justice.

Chris was firmly in the latter group, pulling in old favours and indebting himself to anybody who would accept his promises in return for information on the pirates.

Unfortunately, his quarry were no amateurs, nor were they rum-drinking parrot fanciers. They were twenty-first century criminals, connected to an underworld at least as sprawling and complex as the legitimate world it lurked below.

Satellite archive showed a large, decrepit junk, making its way towards the Farm. It had left the Yellow Sea and headed out towards the Farm at a slow cruise, in full accordance with its dilapidated demeanour. From the intercept course, it was clear that it knew exactly where it was going. With the arrival of cloud cover, the images had become vague and noisy. It had not been possible to track the boat's progress further, but its arrival could be inferred from the timing of the RF jamming and electronic warfare attack on the Farm's systems. Video from the Farm was also useless; any systems that hadn't been hacked before the ship had even crossed the horizon were scrambled by EMP and dazzled by lamps. During the four-hour blackout, the pirates had stolen a fortune of tuna, which they had piled on the junk's deck under a mound of ice using the Farm's equipment and their own crane.

They had also added eight, high-value whores to their

catch—and Stella. Once the cloud cleared, more blurry images showed the boat powering away, all pretence at decrepitude dropped.

The satellites had lost sight of the junk again under another thick blanket of cloud. Switching to infrared video recordings hadn't helped; somehow, it could mask its heat signature. Seven hours later, the drifting, unregistered junk had been picked up by the Nipponese coastguard.

Chris had later received an update: the hull had been a disguise. A conning tower had poked up into the wheelhouse, and the pirate submersible had worn the junk like a mask. The best guess was that the vessel was trickled-down military surplus. It explained how such a knackered old wreck had made such good progress, while emitting so little infrared radiation. They were lucky to have captured the shabby craft; minutes later, it would have sunk, taking precious information with it.

The DNA the Nipponese had swept from its decks gave them a start, but apart from that, the news was grim. The hostages had probably already been transferred to another vessel. Similar crimes, although none so audacious, had been popping up over the past months and had a connection to the Cartel—the massive, shadowy, tentacled monster and bastard child of every pre-Mesh mafia-style group. The Kinfolk might label themselves White Hats, but the Cartel would not choose Black. In all likelihood, given a choice of headwear, they would probably select surgical caps and dental face shields.

Chris felt a terrible weight on his shoulders. An ex-military Cartel stealth sub would be virtually impossible to detect from orbit or from the air. There were so many small vessels swarming the islands and straights that a pirate crew wouldn't have a problem slinking off to some quiet port to offload their booty.

```
[Offline Message] @2@k1 has sent a message.
"Mr. Tucker, I am a friend of Stella [Friendship Certifi-
cate: <additional information>] I heard the news on GNN.
Perhaps I can help. Ping me back on this address when you
get a chance."
```

Chris let the message scroll across his Spex and then glanced at Marcel to make sure there was no change in the rhythm of the boy's breathing. He pulled out his Companion to answer and tapped away on the tiny keyboard. Imagining how Stella would have made fun of him for that old-fashioned habit, he forced a cough from what would otherwise have been a sob. Almost as soon as he had sent his response, a second message appeared requesting a live session, and a window popped up on his Spex.

The boy looked to be about seventeen or eighteen, long dark hair tied back in a ponytail, with a hooked nose and olive skin. He wore a brown leather jacket over a red lumberjack shirt.

Chris wouldn't usually accept unsolicited comms, but he had set his spam filter to its most tolerant level, so as not to block any potential leads.

"Thanks for taking this call," said the boy. "Stella has talked a lot about you. I'm not sure if she ever mentioned me or my brother, but we want to help in any way we can."

"Hi Zaki. Yes, Stella talks about you sometimes. It's going to be all right. Don't worry, we're doing everything we can to find her."

"Yeah, sure. Me and my Kin are busy, too, so I won't talk for long. Stella obviously trusted you, and you seem to be legit, so I thought I would pass on what we know. Hopefully, you will get back to us if you get any leads from your end?"

"Sure, that sounds fair. Go on."

"We managed to get some information on the sub. It looks like it might be heading to San Herando in the Philippines. There is a big Russ factory ship moored up there. It's possible they are planning to transfer the tuna into the ship's freezers."

The boy looked off camera, giving Chris the impression he was assimilating new data as he spoke. "As I said, Stella talked a lot about you, Mr Tucker. She mentioned you used to be in the navy. Maybe you can pull some strings to get some boots on the ground there, in case they offload Stella?"

"Can you back any of this up? I don't want to waste time on a wild-goose chase."

"I'm sending over a tarball with all the source data. Take a look."

Chris okayed the incoming bulk data transfer request. He was stunned. When he saw the kid, he had silently cursed himself for letting the call through. He had expected to play the role of stoic older father-figure, offering platitudes to a heart-broken teenage crush. Instead, in a few concise statements, the boy confirmed the theories of half a dozen experts and provided the closest thing to hope Chris had dared experience since the first call.

"The data is coming in now. I'll take a look and get back to you."

"Thanks, Mr Tucker."

"Thank you! How did you get all that stuff?"

"I've got some good friends and so does Stella. They want to help. They found the boat, right? Did you manage to get the DNA they pulled off it?"

"Yeah, four sets."

"Finally, some good news. Can you send it over?"

Chris nodded.

***

They exchanged weary smiles, and Zaki cut the connection. He kept a frozen frame of Chris from the video link and added metadata before filing it away with the rest of the research.

He stared towards infinity, looking through the bloody puncture in the plaster by the door, flexing the fingers of his right hand, while massaging his knuckles. He had been furious with his mother for not letting him take their Land Voyager and set off immediately to Stella's rescue. She was right, of course. As a family, they had once travelled thousands of kilometres across Anatolia and the Balkans, but he would need to cover twelve times that; and, even if he survived a journey across a dozen countries—several knee-deep in anarchy of their own—it would take him months to get to the Philippines. Stella would be long gone by then; the trail would be cold. It had been a stupid idea.

Zaki knew that wanting to dash halfway across the world had been a childish physical reaction. He missed his dad. Anosh would have taken charge. He would have come up with a plan. They would probably have found Stella by now.

Staring at the bloody hole he had punched in the wall, he almost lost it again, furious at the universe for taking first his father and now his friend.

He managed to bite it down. He knew the universe was empty of meaning. Huge, fascinating, and pointless. He might as well get angry at a brick. Anyway, he was a cripple. What good would he do hobbling around, dragging his foot, pointing a gun with his cramped, twisted hand? The best place for him was online. Like his Silicium Kin, he was a digital ninja, perfectly adapted to his environment. Last-generation satellites and networked security cameras were theirs to own. He could pull live feed from across the globe and listen into everything but the most encrypted military traffic. He would find the pirates, and when he did they wouldn't know what had hit them.

Code had become a commodity. None of the established players really wrote software anymore. The Mesh's seething ecosystem of FAC produced code a hundred times faster and a thousand times cheaper than the cubicle farms of the crumbling corporate remnants. It was usually easier just to 'borrow' or steal. Even ostensibly professional engineers took shortcuts. Systems ended up as composite monsters, full of spliced-together snippets and modules miscellaneously sourced from projects found floating innocently through the aether.

Plasmids; Trojan modules worming their way into purportedly secure systems, creating chimeras riddled with compromised code. Backdoors patiently waiting for the return of their masters.

Zaki snapped out of his musings and went to find his brother, who was ensconced in the big shed, putting the finishing touches to their latest weaponised mini drone: a tiny stealthed disk a little larger than a frisbee, fitted with solid state, multi-barrel, micro guns. The drone was as far removed from their first cute little quad-copter, with its stink bombs and laser pointers, as the Kitty Hawk was from a sixth-generation fighter.

The combat drone was small and light, loaded out with both explosive rounds and flechettes tipped with ampoules of box jellyfish venom that the boys had brewed up in one of the smaller bioreactors. They would need feet on the ground at some point and, although Zaki was hoping Chris could help, they were also putting together a Plan B and a care package to increase their options once the shooting started—because there would be shooting. People were going to die. The boys had pledged this to each other and the universe.

Zaki waited impatiently, watching the hover test. When he could wait no longer, he started badgering Siegfried to come and pester their mother with him.

"Come on, bro. Mum's still pissed off with me about last

night. You ask."

"You really think we need three?"

"Yes. I have put together a rough plan. You can take a look later and see if you can strip anything out, but we need one to carry all this." Zaki waved his hand at the assortment of vicious-looking kit lying around on the wooden benches. "And we need at least two others for penetrators."

"*If* we can find her!"

"Don't worry about that, Segs," Zaki said with an edge to his voice that made Segi shiver.

"Okay, I'll ask Mum."

Siegfried landed the drone and plugged it in to charge. Once he was finished, he shoved Zaki in the back to knock him out of his trance. Zaki's mind had drifted out to sea again. Siegfried saw his brother's Spex flickering as he watched feeds from satellites and reviewed messages from the thousands of people now connected to the search.

"Thanks," said Zaki. "The DNA sequences have arrived. I'll plug them into the BugNet."

Segi left the cool shade of the barn and crossed the dusty yard to where their mother was changing the water of some olives she was preserving. Siegfried slipped into the kitchen and watched for a few seconds until she noticed him.

"What?" she asked, feigning irritation to hide any sympathy. She could imagine only too well how she would feel if one of them had been abducted; but, equally, she was terrified they would somehow get sucked in and she would lose another of her men.

"Zaki is sorry about last night, Mum," Segi said.

She turned to look at him, tears in her eyes again. "Oh, tell him it's okay. I know you just want to help your friend. I feel terrible, too."

"Mum, can we use some of the time from the delivery kites, maybe a few weeks?" he asked, taking the opportunity. "We need to get some reconnaissance equipment down there to look for Stella."

"I'm sure the police are doing everything they can, darling."

Since Anosh had died, Ayşe had been forced to learn a lot—everything from how to maintain a wind-turbine to how to birth a baby goat. She lived in a strange mental space between two worlds: she might live on a rural farm, but her children genetically engineered animals and built robots in her barn. It had become commonplace for GliderKites to be delivering eggs or lamb chops one day, and shipping exotic chemicals fabbed in the boys' bioreactors to somewhere as far afield as Cairo and Athens the next.

"Mum!" Segi breathed, exasperated.

Consciously, she accepted these new realities. However, in her heart, she lived back in the twentieth century, a world in which the old rules applied and the police would find a missing girl.

"Oh, I really don't know. We need them for our deliveries…"

"We could upgrade our subscription for this month," he suggested. From the softening of her tone, Siegfried knew it was only a matter of time until his mother conceded.

***

"Bastards!" Chris swore, hurling his tablet across the room, where it bounced off the door and rattled down onto the floor. As a further provocation, the face on its screen continued speaking, and he could still hear the earnest words coming out of its little speakers. He had sent the DNA to the boy Zaki, and had felt some trace of optimism. Finally, they might be making progress. Then he had joined a meeting with the Nipponese-holding company that ran the Farm—

The VP had patiently explained they were not employees, or even the dependents of employees. They were illegal squatters and, in one sense, they had been lucky that they had been allowed to live rent-free for so long…

—that is when Chris had lost it and flung his tablet at the wall.

The kidnap was a crime committed on the high seas outside the jurisdiction of any government. Insurance had already paid for the lost tuna and, as far as they were concerned, the incident was over. It had been a similar story in the morning; he had hoped the Sultan of Kuala Lumpur might want to assist, just for the publicity, maybe putting a SpecOps team on standby for an exciting, telegenic hostage rescue, but it seemed the PR capital from a bunch of orphan whores was not significant enough to justify the expense. Chris was on his own. Although they had been helpful so far, he couldn't count on the two kids or their gaming club; this was the real world, not MinxyMouse!

***

The room was pitch dark and stank of diesel and faeces. Stella could tell by the way the sobbing echoed that they were in a small space. The air was hot, but the walls were cold. Water vapour was permanently condensing onto them and running down to join the filthy slop she found herself sitting in. Raw, welded metal seams ran down the walls and across the floor, adding to the general discomfort. The only positive point she could think of after a prolonged search for a bright side was that it was so filthy and cramped that it was unlikely there would be any raping in the girls' immediate future.

She must have slept because she woke. The door was being opened and a flickering blue light highlighted its elliptical edges before flooding into the cell. The other girls were waking and cringing away from this change in their circumstance. The sobbing started again. Stella realised that one of the voices was her own and immediately stopped the pathetic mewling.

They were ushered out of the two-by-two metre cell and up a ladder towards a blinding light, which turned out to be the afternoon sunlight diffusing through an overcast sky. Stella was disorientated. She remembered being led down into the belly of a traditional Çin junk before being locked into the cell; but now, she had climbed back up the same steps and was standing on a convex deck floating only a few centimetres above the waves. It appeared that most of the boat was lurking below the surface like an iceberg.

A rusty but sleek modern vessel was moored alongside, and it was from a hose attached to this new arrival that a sudden jet of frigid water erupted, blasting into the knot of cringing girls. Stella expected jeers and leers, but the crew was preoccupied with transferring an endless succession of sleek, partially frozen tuna from a hatch at the front of the sunken vessel to the new ship and seemed too busy to be interested in the girls.

Stella's mind took the disinterest as a further positive component term in the complex rape likelihood equation that her mind was running. They were unceremoniously hosed down, and then guns were waved, indicating they should cross a wooden plank and join the frozen tuna on the new vessel.

Across the plank, the atmosphere changed. The new crew looked Hispanic, rather than Çin, and very unsavoury. There was also significantly more leering, which was not a good sign. The girls were ushered aft by a big man with an eyepatch and scarred face, to a cabin with two bunk beds and a small en-suite toilet and shower.

The door shut with a clank. Stella and the others were too listless to confirm it had been locked. Slumped down onto the floor, or sitting on the edges of the bed, a thin sobbing started again. Nobody seemed able to talk. Stella had taken a perch on the end of the bottom bunk and, after an indeterminate period of staring out of the porthole, she saw the submarine drift away and sink even lower into the water, until only the tip of its tower projected above the waves.

That night, the door flew open and three girls were dragged out. Later, faint cries muffled by heavy metal bulkheads and a distant rhythmic percussion confirmed Stella's worst fears. This time, she didn't try to stop herself as she became part of the choir of desperate sobbing that, once more, spread around their little room.

Water slashed from the sky, drilling against the glass skins of skyscrapers packed so densely that they jutted from the earth like the bristles on a brush. The water slid in sheets across slanting surfaces. As it neared the ground, it splashed off neon signs, throwing out garish halos that hung in the misty spray. At street level, it washed the grime off bamboo shelters. On the tarpaulin roofs of street stalls, it gathered in stretched pools that hung like huge pendulous breasts. The rain washed debris from the city's streets along gutters and into the labyrinth of drains below.

Her little mind knew it was a good time to forage in the newly deposited flotsam, but there was another reason she waited here. Long ago, while she lay, her eyes newly opened, her mother had brought food. Although small and hard, impossible to chew and difficult to swallow, it was delicious. Something in its taste and smell made the tiny grub of a rat she had been, persevere. Finally, she had managed to gulp it down. Now, standing slightly out of the torrent that crashed through the grating above, with her whiskers twitching in anticipation, she felt a nagging compulsion to find more.

She waited. She knew food would come soon; she could taste it in the water. She waited with two of her sisters and a stranger from another litter. They all felt the same urge. The knowledge of imminent food was becoming more intense, stronger, nearer, when suddenly the smell she remembered from long ago was all around her. One of her sisters darted forward, disappearing into the wall of water; lost for a few seconds, she came back holding something small and hard in her mouth and immediately ran off.

Her own sharp eyes focused on a second dot in the riot of water, and she leapt into the cataract to retrieve it. Disappointment; her teeth bit into spongy nicotine-soaked paper, and she let the stub wash out of her mouth. But now, in the water, she could taste it near. Diving to the bottom, she nosed around on the slick concrete. A small collection of debris was gathered together by the swirling currents, and, in the middle, a small ball surrounded by an intoxicating taste.

Seconds later, she was out of the water and dashing back along the tunnel to where her own babies waited, wriggling against each other in the dark. She shivered, shaking the water off her fur before squeezing through into the crack where she had made her nest. She dropped the capsule and nudged what she had already decided was the strongest of her offspring towards it. She watched and mewed, encouraging the little mite as its misplaced suckle reflex fixed the object in its toothless mouth. It tried to suck on the capsule, but seemed to find it rough and unpleasant. The mother patiently nudged it back to its mouth and, after several failed attempts, a random push rotated the black lozenge. On the next attempt, the tiny scales on its surface caught in the soft tissue of the little rat's mouth. The capsule was big and difficult to swallow, but tasted good. After nearly exhausting itself gulping down the food, the little creature nudged around blindly, looking for its mother, but she had already gone compulsively back to the drain and the promise of more beads.

Over the next few days, the mucus shell slowly dissolved in the juices of the baby's stomach, revealing glass barbs that lodged in the epithelial lining of the baby's intestine.

It held it fast and, soon, the strange little glass ball began to ooze a haze of enzymes and hormones. These biological urgings tricked its host's body into encysting it and drawing it through the stomach lining. As months passed, the little baby grew into an inquisitive young rodent. The thing in its belly called forth blood vessels to encircle it and sent out fibrous ganglia into the young rat's spine. Through these new nerves, it began sending signals, which the developing brain learnt to interpret. The stimuli hijacking its nervous system was soon accepted as sensory input, and it would eventually recognise the foreign desires and intentions as its own.

'Danger near; movement behind wall; enemy approaching'

***

Conflict is the natural state of man and nature. Every creature fighting against all others for its right to live and breed. Nature is war; all against all.

Only the tight bonds of kin align individuals into groups: clans, packs or nests.

The development of complex human societies compart-mentalised this violence. Specialised warrior castes and standing armies came to fight the battles. War was limited. Murder and hardship may follow defeat, but for most of written history, war would leave the agrarian life of the peasants untouched.

Industrialisation brought a third development, the concept of "Total War". An entire country or empire mobilised and focused on the single goal of obliterating the enemy.

Nothing was sacred from Total War. No one was safe from firebombs or atomic destruction.

By the end of the twentieth century, global webs of interdependencies had made these grand, world-spanning conflagrations inefficient. The country your hard-line generals were urging you to nuke was probably the ancestral home of a significant percentage of your citizens, or your prime supplier of labour, oil, or any of the hundreds of other strategically critical resources within the Gordian knot of global trade.

Fourth-generation warfare was about asymmetry: partisans, terrorists, and plausibly deniable special operators.

By the third decade of the twenty-first century, the fifth generation of warfare had arrived. No dense treatise was required to unravel its principles; it was simply that the majority of combatants were now non-human.

***

Zaki had uploaded the DNA swept from the abandoned pirate boat. Chris had already dispatched it to the Cartel botnets, and had bid as much as he could afford for the location of the nameless individuals the DNA encoded. Yet, the boys knew that Russ factory ships, stolen submarines, and large-scale tuna rustling painted a picture with Cartel prints all over it and that, however distributed and chaotic, the Cartel was hardly likely to deliver intel on its own operations.

Fortunately, the Cartel was only one of the leviathans sliding beneath the surface of the dark-net sea. The Clans were powerful, too. Fragments of their open source code, riddled with backdoor vulnerabilities, were scattered like buckshot through the world's computer networks.

Few people knew the reach of the Mesh or suspected its weakly omnipotent capabilities. Less were aware that huge orders for cryptic hardware were regularly placed at medical chip fabricators across the globe. Coin changed hands, records were modified. Factories, built to fabricate DNA-sequencing chips, or cognitive prosthetics, spent long, undocumented maintenance cycles turning out endless batches of small glass beads stuffed with obscure configurations of radios and processors. Secrecy surrounding these unusual, ingestible neuro-interface chips was maintained with threats, favours, or straight up bribery. Even at the top of the Clans, there was heated speculation; somebody must be funding the massive ongoing expense needed to research, design and manufacture each new design iteration...

Thousands of the small glass beads ended up flushed down toilets, scattered into drains, or cast onto rubbish tips every day. Every bead eaten by a compatible host added another nervous system to the BugNet.

The newest versions could sniff traces of DNA from the contents of a host's stomach, snap faces from the traffic passing through its optic nerves, or detect hundreds of compounds by monitoring the host animal's olfactory lobes. The information was shared across the BugNet, wirelessly bouncing between cybernetically enhanced vermin, until it was picked up by a MeshNode.

Typical to the hacker win-win ethic, the relationship was

symbiotic; the selective advantage of being able to sense the beating of a cat's heart through a brick wall, or 'smell' which wires carried power, or squeak a warning that a similarly endowed nest mate hundreds of metres away could hear, ensured there was an ever-growing number of hosts who actively sought the helpful little glass beads. It also didn't hurt that they tasted delicious.

Most end users would never know where their sought-after intelligence came from, but the Kinfolk's ability to find a missing body buried under tons of rotting fish on a dump, or a fugitive hiding in a filthy hut in an off-grid slum, gave them an almost supernatural reputation in the underworld.

To the brothers, growing up physically isolated from eligible female representation, Stella had always been more than a node in the Clan's web of useful contacts. Since their first incorporeal meeting, she had been a fascination to both adolescent boys.

When–like now–Zaki closed *his* eyes, he could see hers. Vast and sorrowful; pulling at his insides, like a swallowed hook pulling him down into their deep, dark pools.

They could also transform within a blink into bright exclamation points for her dazzling, incapacitating, smile–filling his form with transcendent light, lifting his soul above the clouds...

He knew she preferred Segi. He wasn't surprised. He had come to accept it. Anyway, she made Zaki uncomfortable to the point that he behaved like a dick around her most of the time. It didn't matter. It only mattered that they found her.

He blinked and spammed another message to the SOS thread on the Silicium forums. He was trying to wheedle altruism from benevolent SuperUsers, persuading them to donate identity and reputation to Zaki's BugNet search.

***

Pedro took the beer from the tray, while eyeing the ass of their curvaceous waitress. He winked across the table to another of his crew, almost the stereotypical pirate; a huge man with a scar, eyepatch, tied-back hair and, beneath the table, a vicious knife strapped to his ankle. They were vaguely drunk. They had stopped here, in this desperately poor part of New Guinea, to pick up the last of the new meat before setting out for the West Coast of the US, where young Asian flesh pulled in punters bored with a staple diet of small-town runaway white trash.

The new girls waited, tied together with hemp rope, in a small shack half a dozen metres away from where Pedro and his two shipmates were sitting, drinking their beers. Out over the bamboo rail, two hundred metres offshore, the lights of his boat glittered reassuringly. They had cruised for a week from the last pickup and would lie up for a few more days, sorting out fuel and food for the next, much longer, leg of their journey.

Once they had the new cargo safely locked in with the previous batch, Pedro's unsavoury band would settle in for an evening of heavy drinking, followed by a bit of recreational raping.

The door banged open and a stocky, dark-skinned tribal came barrelling in. He wore a tattered pair of tourist's safari shorts and a flowery shirt, but his face was symmetrically scarred in a very un-tourist-like way. A bone pierced his nose. In his hand, a short axe hung from loosely clenched fingers. His eyes darted across the room, skipping from table to table, ignoring farmers and thugs, but stopping on Pedro. A look of livid recognition crossing his face, the newcomer barged past protesting customers and headed directly for the pirates.

He was a powerful man, but Pedro didn't feel threatened. There were three of them, and the man didn't seem armed with anything that would trump the Uzi hanging from a strap under Pedro's stained canvas jacket. The man reached them and, while they were still calmly getting to their feet, he grabbed the rim of their table and violently hurled it towards them. Glasses and bottles, sent flying as the table was assaulted, rained down on the startled pirates. They had to jump back to avoid debris and were now pressed against the hut's wall. Usually a bar fight would take a while to warm up, leaving plenty of time to humiliate and slowly kill whoever had been stupid enough to try them, but this time the ferocity of the attack had caught them by surprise.

Fragments of broken glass had showered Pedro's face. He tasted blood as it dripped down over his lip from a deep cut in the side of his nose. Even while the glass was tinkling onto the wooden floor, Pedro was drawing his machine pistol. Before any follow-up attack could be launched, and with the gun still on the upswing, he opened up with an appalling flaming roar. Bullets walked up the man's chest, from left thigh to right shoulder, smashing him back. Some lodged in the floor or smashed glasses on the tables behind the black-skinned local.

Miraculously, nobody else was hit. The sounds of broken glass and spent shells clattering to the floor faded, leaving the room in a stunned silence. The unused axe slid impotently from between relaxing fingers.

The three pirates looked around menacingly, but the man seemed to have been alone; nobody showed any interest in helping him as he lay, bubbling and gasping, on the floor. Pedro put his hand to his own face, then took out a nasty serrated blade from its sheath in the small of his back. He inspected the damage to his nose in its reflection and, satisfied it was nothing serious, grinned at his shipmates.

"We fight, and then we fuck! Let me look at this pig. I wish to recognise his daughter later!"

The two returned his massive roar of laughter. Cold eyes looked to the overturned chairs and broken bottles and then towards a neighbouring table. The panicked group at the unaffected table quickly cleared away and generously offered their seats. Soon, fresh beers had arrived. The body was dragged out and dumped onto the sand for the dogs or the tide.

Around midnight they left, dragging the human chain of whimpering cargo with them. None of the locals raised a finger as they ferried them out to their boat floating in the bay.

Feeling sick, despite years of numbness, the owner watched the boat's lights recede. He told the waitress to go home, then pulled a full bottle of rum from under the bar and sat with a couple of the regulars to drink thought away.

In silence they drank. At 4 am, the last of the customers staggered out and down the rough-hewn wooden steps. Already barely conscious, the owner let his head fall onto the bar and passed out. The waitress, who was also the maid, accountant, and cook, was long gone. There was nobody to sweep up the fallen nuts and broken glass.

While the owner drooled on the scarred wood, dozens of tiny sharp claws skittered along the bar, across the floor, and under the tables. The little army of rodents collected the edible debris. One bright pair of eyes licked at some sticky residue coating a shard of broken glass: sweet beer and rich, red drops of protein.

In its stomach, acids began to digest the food, absorbing sugars and proteins, assimilating what had once been pirate and would soon be mouse—but, before the little mammal's metabolism had a chance to complete its job, very un-rodent-like enzymes were working at the traces of DNA they had found in the pirate's blood. They cut it into fragments of easily sequenceable length, ready for the millions of pits studding the surface of a little glass bead meshed beside the mouse's stomach.

DNA was ingested, analysed, and sequenced. Data was encrypted and broadcast to the mouse's neighbours, hopping from body to body across the BugNet. Mouse to rat, rat to crow, crow to monkey. It took two days and a hundred hosts before the packets reached the Mesh.

Less than a second later, an alarm vibrated through the Spex which were lying on a table next to Zaki's bed. Not even half awake, he reached out his hand, fumbling in the dark to check the message.

Chapter 8 – Lost Action Hero

His phantom foot no longer hurt. The psychiatrists told him his brain was doing okay, too. He didn't really feel like letting anyone know that he was on the mend, though, so he kept himself glued to the screen, watching the bland and repetitive programming the hospital piped to the patients' rooms.

The place smelt of detergent. The bed had a mattress that could hinge him up into a sitting position, or let him lie flat. He hated it. The motor sound and the feeling of an irresistible force posing his body like a manikin was too familiar, too likely to induce flashbacks of being confined within his hated battlesuit.

The other wrecked young men he shared his days with were mostly too medicated or shell-shocked to be good company. The nurses were bland and repetitive, old and jaded, but he had warmed to their no-nonsense bustling affection. They were unflappable and he had relied on that matter-of-fact attitude on the few occasions when he had lost it for a while, or needed fluids cleaned up.

The blinds were half down. Outside, it would be dark soon. The sun was reflecting in great orange flashes from the windows of the opposite wing. Keith was watching a film. A tray with plastic crockery and the remains of his bland and repetitive meal rested on his lap. It was basically a children's story, unlikely to tip the viewers into frenzied flashback insanity, but it was vaguely exciting. At least, it had people in it, not just animals. Keith suspected they were trying him out on harder stuff to see if he was getting better. He thought about feigning a screaming rage to make sure they got no ideas about kicking him out, or sending him back to work. A colonel, who had visited early in his stay, had dispelled any ideas of medical discharge when he had cheerily explained that losing a foot was not a major impediment to a soldier in these days of assisted exoskeletons. He had added that, if Keith signed up for another five years, his pension should even cover a real lab-grown foot—his own cartilage and stem cells printed in zero-g in orbital organ factories.

The phone rang.

"Receive call," said Keith to the room.

The film paused and a dark, blurry shot of a face topped by a big mop of dark hair appeared.

"Keith Wilson?"

"Yes?"

"Err, we would like to offer you a job."

"A job!?" Keith sniggered at the very idea. "You must have the wrong number!"

Another voice joined the conversation, leaning briefly in front of the cam. "He said your name, bud! How the fuck could it be a wrong number?"

"Shut up! We agreed I should do the talking!"

Keith stared at the display at the end of his bed. "Fuck! Are you kids? Wait… I know you, don't I?"

"Yeah, you know us," continued the voice off-screen. "We're the people who recently saved your life when you were about to be captured and tortured to death by ZKF separatists. And now, it's your turn. We need your help, okay?"

"We have money," tried the first voice. "But look, a friend is in trouble, and we need... we really need you to help."

"Bad luck. You know you are calling me in a looney bin, right? They tell me I'm in no fit state to help anybody."

"Our friend. She's been kidnapped by pirates."

"Pirates?" Keith muttered.

"Yeah, fucking pirates, and not Jolly Roger types looking for buried treasure. These are the psychotic, sadistic, kidnapper types looking for fresh white flesh to traffic."

"We really need your help."

Their faces pixelated and froze as connection glitches smeared them into a psychedelic blocky mess. Keith got the warning peel of tinnitus that often announced a PTSD flashback. His vision became a tunnel…

…the grasshopper bounces in front like a karaoke dot leading him onwards. When he rests, or passes out, it waits for him patiently. He limps and then crawls through the day. His foot is numb. He can smell something nasty over the taint of burnt rubber and roasted pork. He sleeps under a tree.

In the morning, the insect is still there, looking at him with its alien slanting eyes. They set off again, the locust hopping on ahead, while he follows at his own pathetic pace. By the middle of the morning, a little group of buildings appears in a small valley between two low hills. The grasshopper pauses dramatically; then, spreading its wings, it flies off towards them. It quickly disappears in the wavering heated air. Keith staggers the remaining five hundred metres, then falls into the dust. Before he passes out for the final time, he notices a woman standing in the shadow of a doorway...

He hadn't seen much of the family. They had clearly manufactured it that way. The woman, who spoke some English, ignored all questions relating to mysterious insects. The old crone who brought him his meals—foul-tasting teas and delicious bowls of stew—didn't speak at all.

They treated him well, despite his babbling and the occasional night-time screaming fit, when sanity was cast aside by the pain in his festering leg. Unsurprisingly, the damaged flesh had continued to get worse. They had given him antibiotics, which cleared his fever, but did little against the incinerated, rotting lump of flesh hanging off the bottom of his shin.

After about a week, they took him on a bus. By then, he was feverish and incoherent again. They drove for what seemed like days, each pothole or bump in the road sending agonising shocks up his leg and, through his bones, into his brain. When they arrived, they had bundled him into a taxi and given the driver a wad of paper. The taxi driver half-carried him into the British consulate in Ankara and dumped him unceremoniously in the middle of a large, crowded hall. Hundreds of people jostled between queues that seemed to form and dissolve spontaneously. The crowd, gaining a new direction, recoiled from his smell and ravings, leaving a clear space around him.

He had spent the next few weeks in a Caliphate hospital outside Ankara. Despite only having a hazy memory of the entire episode, he recalled clearly the experience of no longer having a foot. He remembered them changing his bandage. The mess was not a pretty sight; thick black stitches closed off the flesh of his lower leg like a trussed joint of meat, and the whole area was sticky with a bright orange gel he assumed kept the ghastly wound germ-free.

The British army flew him home. Later, they confirmed he had been the only survivor from the terrorist attack on his squad. Until he had miraculously shown up again, he had been assumed vaporised in the crash, or dragged off and eaten by wild animals.

His miracle survival had been paraded briefly in front of an attention-deficit media, and then he was sent to the sanatorium to convalesce.

He had nearly forgotten the two teenage boys he had watched from his window as they came and went, chattering together in what sounded like Prussian. His saviours had obviously not wanted anybody to know they had been involved in the rescue of an enemy soldier. He didn't mention them, claiming amnesia instead, and jabbering from time to time about a grasshopper.

Keith rubbed his eyes. The two boys had disappeared from

the screen and had been replaced by a picture that took him a couple of seconds to figure out. Once the perspective clicked, it resolved as a boat seen from above. The sun was shining brightly on the white V of its wake, and glinting from metal objects in its superstructure. The picture shimmered like a desert mirage, hazy and unsteady. He reasoned that he was most likely watching video from a satellite. Then, the view unexpectedly zoomed, until the ship took up the whole screen. It was blocky and often out of focus, but Keith could make out men walking around the deck, holding black objects. From the way they were carried, it was clear they were weapons.

"This is live," came the voice of one of the boys. "Our friend is on that boat with at least eight other kidnapped girls. The bastards took her from her home, murdered her friends, and God knows what they have been doing to her on that ship!"

Keith was suddenly sober: this was real. In a world full of scams and phishing and relentless media spin, this was real. An abducted girl was on that boat—the boat he was looking at.

"Kids, that's tough. But there is nothing I can do. I am in your debt, and I'll make it up any way I can, but I'm locked away in here. I'm not even allowed calls. I had an episode once I got back to England. I made a scene. They call this place a military hospital, but it's more like a mental asylum. Just talking to you like this will bring down a ton of trouble any second. I don't know what's taking them so long actually..."

"We've got this, bro. The nurses think you're asleep. It's all cool. We fixed it!" Then, the other boy pushed back onto the screen. "We know you. You have the skills. Please?"

"Guys! I'm locked up. If those pics are recent, then you need someone half a fucking world away!"

The younger kid, still in front of the camera, continued speaking to Keith.

"If you're in, we've got this. We can fix all of that."

***

Keith closed his eyes. The plane was finally moving, taxiing from the terminal, taking a complex route through the maze of tarmac towards the runway. He was sitting in First Class, which took up over half of the double-decker plane. Tax and carbon offset credits made air travel so astronomically expensive these days that it made little difference to the airline's running costs if the chairs were made of leather or plastic, or if the forks were disposable or silver-plated. There were probably something like twelve coach class seats squashed up next to the toilets, whose only purpose was to allow the first and business travellers to feel superior to someone. These would have been heavily marketed at an attainable price and had, almost certainly, been gobbled up only minutes after becoming bookable.

Keith felt moderately calm for the first time since the boys had hung up the call sixteen hours ago.

The door to his room in the hospital had been inexplicably unlocked, and the orderly had been nowhere in sight. As instructed, Keith had pulled on his recently issued high-tech rubber foot and simply walked out through the deserted kitchen. It was 11.45 pm; no food would be prepared until the next morning. The delivery door at the back was also unlocked. He was not challenged as he pushed it open and climbed the stained concrete steps. At the wall that surrounded the grounds, he had needed to improvise for the first and last time, but managed to scramble up a tree and drop safely down the other side, nearly spraining his organic ankle.

He had been told confidently not to worry about the usually omniscient gaze of the security cameras that perched, like an enormous flock of starlings, on every compatible surface of the hospital's walls and roofs. According to plan, a cab should be waiting at a church a few minutes' walk away.

His years in the military had prepared him for the inevitability of every apparently foolproof plan failing almost immediately, usually leaving chaos and inconvenient piles of dead bodies. His respect for these two kids was approaching reverence as he easily picked out the steeple towering above the other buildings and navigated towards it.

The cab was there as promised. Its lights flicked on as he approached, and it chirped cheerfully as he placed his thumb on the little bio-pad on the passenger door. The destination was already programmed and, without complaint, it drove him the three hours it took to reach the airport hotel. The drive was uneventful, and the cab's entertainment system provided adequate company.

He didn't even need to remember a room number; another thumb scanner on the lobby door, ignorant of its error, recognised him as one Nathan Nicol and popped open the main door. A breadcrumb trail of little green lights appeared in the centre of the carpet, dancing off towards room 183. Another biometric exchange at the room door and he was in, surrounded by luxuries such as towels, fruit, and a television that could probably be instructed to display content more explicit than Gruffle Puffle re-runs.

He had woken up nine hours later, clad in a hotel bathrobe, surrounded by miniature bottles of vodka and whisky. The television was still on and endlessly looping. Keith became momentarily distracted from his headache by the action on the screen. The film—in the spirit of plausible deniability, stretching commonly accepted definitions to breaking point—might be described as a fly-on-the-wall documentary set in a nurses' school, its loose narrative following the unexpectedly exciting lives of a local pizza delivery man and a window cleaner...

The door's chime had woken him. He hastily cleared away the evidence of his solo party before opening it to a smiling bellboy holding a large AladdinsCave™ emblazoned cardboard box. The box had been stuffed full of goodies, including a complete set of clothes, underwear, hiking boots, a new tablet Companion, a pair of Spex, a wallet (dismayingly empty), an umbrella, a rain jacket and a nice rucksack.

Keith had showered and dressed in his new clothes, stuffing his white mental asylum pyjamas into the rucksack for later disposal, then opened the door of his room to face the world.

***

The plane finished its taxiing and stopped at the end of

the runway, waiting for a small, blended-wing luxury jet in front to roar into the sky. Keith took his new wallet and passport out of the seat pocket and cast his incredulous gaze over them once more. The documents and the other contents of his bulging wallet had been hand-delivered by an Otaku bicycle messenger as he waited at the big, automatic doors of check-in zone five.

In the hotel room, he had used his new Companion to enter the Mesh address that his teenage operators had forced him to memorise back at the hospital.

Tapton04111998.mesh

They were obviously not very impressed with his mental abilities. The URL had simply been the town where he had lived as a child, followed by his date of birth. He had been greeted with an idiot-proof set of instructions for downloading a custom OS onto both Spex and Companion. Once this was accomplished, the tablet auto-connected and two grinning faces, obviously massively pleased with themselves, had appeared on the screen. Secure communication channel established, he had become little more than a marionette following the instructions or arrows that his Spex caused to appear in his field of vision, listening to hyperenergetic explanations of how cool and almost impossibly difficult all this had been.

Keith gathered that they'd had some help, at least financially—which had made things like having a shrink-wrapped envelope stuffed with fresh credit cards and a passport pressed into his hands by a green-haired elf in a mini-skirt—seem less like the delusions of a crazy, shell-shocked veteran. Even so, Keith wasn't 100% convinced of the integrity of his mind. He wouldn't have been surprised to wake up, still in his hospital crib, with his arms firmly secured to the metal bars.

The whining of the engines rose to a distant roar and he was pressed back into his seat as the big old whale began lumbering down the runway, starting its long journey towards Hawai'i.

A behemoth swallowed down the ocean. Eddies span sedately within its vast, barnacle-encrusted jaws. Occasionally, excited fish would dart out, escaping the relentless flow, spooked by unusual electrical gradients and an unpleasant alkali tang. The little silver flashes of light left the gullet through conveniently placed gill slits two metres tall.

The tattered body of a sea turtle hung from the corner of the mouth, bumping along the monster's cheek as currents pulled at the tangled fuzz-ball of nylon netting and seaweed that had eventually drowned the exhausted creature. Several seagulls perched on the brow, hopping around, jostling for position. They craned heads to stare with intent little eyes at the ribbons of flesh trailing the unfortunate, churning reptile.

The sun glinted from a rusted metal head and from the shield-sized solar scales cresting the back of the mechanical leviathan. Air moving within its network of bladders and tubes farted and hissed. Sequentially pressurised air sacks sent peristaltic waves undulating along the great iron spine.

Its various stomachs were filled with bottles, cans, and shreds of plastic plankton. Over weeks, progressing through its alimentary canal towards its artificial anus, the millions of fragments of drifting debris slowly acquired a growing encrustation of coral, until, ultimately, within the rearmost sections of its synthetic bowel, a solid mass of calcium carbonate matrix packed its pseudo-rectum.

Niato pulled away, his POV quickly rising into the air and revealing the segmented back and translucent flank of the

ScumWhale. Its pale, sinuous body and armoured head made it look like a wood-boring larva, flexing in a puddle after being evicted from the dark safety of its log.

Pulling back further, the curve of the Earth became apparent. Overlays and annotations cluttered his field of view. Hundreds of other ScumWhales were highlighted, some leaving, others returning from months at sea. These converged on Bäna Island, where they would wait until the tide was right, and then the gigantic artificial creatures would swim into the vast pens at the north of the island. Here, wallowing in the warm shallow waters, like metal-headed Ctenophores congregating to spawn, they would void their bowels, letting a chalky gravel settle into the millions of rectangular moulds that lined the floor of the pens. Then, as the tide began to turn, they would head back out to open waters to start their slow journey back to the infinite swirling garbage gyres.

Over several weeks, the plastic-speckled coral gravel would settle and harden as the polyps completed their work, pulling carbon from the water to build their skeletons. The loose bleached stool would eventually solidify into honeycomb blocks of limestone, lightweight and carbon negative. Dried and brushed smooth, the blocks would then be piled into towering walls and pyramids, ready to be taken to the construction projects that had turned much of the jungle paradise into something more reminiscent of an opencast mine.

From a sufficiently elevated perspective, the piles of limestone blocks looked like sugarcube sculptures. At the same scale, the black shapes perched upon them would be chunky tropical ants.

Niato's guests were still a few minutes away, so he zoomed in his POV; the ants resolved into chimpanzees. Twenty or so lounged on blocky bulwarks, many eating oranges. One was jumping animatedly on the back of a trailer, which was empty, apart from a single block. Two other chimps close by, who seemed to be the target of the jumping screamer's agitation, were pointedly ignoring her. A small group of elephants stood nearby, picking distractedly at a few blades of grass.

One of Niato's guilty pleasures was his fascination with the soap opera politics that defined the simple lives of his simian subjects. Giving in to his voyeuristic urges, he decided to use his royal super-user privileges to eavesdrop on the little tableau.

The two chimpanzees, who were now licking the peel of their eviscerated oranges, started paying a modicum of attention to their irate, orange-less, colleague.

'Work; exclamation' YellowHat sent, simultaneous with another vocal scream, whose content was clear across the species divide without translation.

The lounging pair looked away nonchalantly, apparently interested in the horizon.

To an agent participating in the Mesh-mediated consensual hallucination, the lone physical block was accompanied by a trailer full of spectral white cubes. Together, the real and virtual blocks covered the base. Three hovering virtual oranges rotated slowly above the blocks. To further clarify the transaction, the virtual oranges and translucent virtual blocks would intermittently disappear, the blocks reappearing one at a time, until the trailer was virtually full again, at which point the oranges would also pop back into existence, looking juicier and more enticing than ever.

Several trucks were standing empty in the region. It was already late morning. Most of the chimps had already earned their breakfast.

The blocks disappeared again and, one by one, they began to re-materialise. This time, however, after the last block had manifested, instead of the usual orange icons, six oversized virtual cigarettes popped into existence. Instantly, the two orange eaters jumped up and raced towards the trailer. They immediately found blocks and, using their impressive strength, began piling limestone onto the bed of the trailer.

YellowHat looked on with shock and outrage. Clearly, she was more interested in her breakfast than a smoke break. Five other apes had now also raced up to join the fray. Motivated by the promise of nicotine, the apes worked in a frenzy while YellowHat deliberated.

Soon, the trailer was filled. Less than a minute after the last block was stacked, a drone whizzed down out of the air. The chimps went berserk as it distributed the pre-agreed six cigarettes. The share of loot was impeccably fair—two ciggies going to the chimp who had moved the most blocks, the others going to four more happy apes. That left three very pissed-off chimpanzees: two workers with nothing, and YellowHat, who clearly felt she had been betrayed by her drug-addicted colleagues and would now have to load a whole cart herself if she wanted any breakfast.

The empty-handed chimps began to circle their shrieking co-workers, who were holding their prizes high out of reach in anticipation of robbery.

'Negative; stealing; exclamation' the drone sent, flashing its red and blue lights and blaring its siren.

Early on, there had been a lot more violence; however, after running the experiment for several years, the chimps were familiar with the rules. They knew they would lose the right to work the block yard if they caused any trouble.

An elephant broke off from the small herd and used its trunk to pull the harness over its head. It set off, pulling the loaded cart towards Atlantis City, where its reward would be waiting.

Niato again delighted in the different temperaments of the two mammals. The elephants didn't bicker or posture. A few bars of infrasound and the odd stamped foot and the decision of who was to go next was made.

Although they were capable, the elephants rarely used their neural Companions to communicate. They were happy with their own rich, sonorous language. Humans who wanted to join in their moots were expected to converse in the same low-frequency grumbles.

"Hey!" a voice exclaimed, while a hand grabbed his upper arm.

Niato started and instinctively lifted his Spex to see what was up.

A short, wiry man was holding his arm tightly. He was dressed somewhat unusually in a close-fitting white shirt buttoned up to the collar and a tight pair of black trousers with pointy shoes. He was smiling, but little else of his face could be discerned because of the translucent animated plastic mask he wore over his face.

"Spying?" he asked.

"I guess so," Niato replied. "How long have you been there?"

"I just got here. It's looking good!" said the man.

"You think so? I think it looks like a wound!"

"It looks like a bowl of broken eggs. Want to see the omelette?"

"Just one sec." Niato let his Spex fall back down over his eyes. YellowHat was still alone, barely a third of the way through loading another trailer. He again invoked godlike powers and caused the three orange icons to appear prematurely, rewarding the stoic chimp for her persistence.

"You know the way you use your superior intellect to manipulate their primitive urges and trick them into working for you?" said the man. "It's ironically similar to what the Forwards and their Sages are doing, don't you think? And, if I remember, it's one of the main reasons you persuaded us to build this city in the first place."

"It's not the same," Niato replied defensively. "This is fair. The chimps are happy with the deal. And so are the high-IQ, highly paid, primate advocates we employ to make sure we are not pandering to any baser urges. This is the Golden Rule. We are treating them as we would want to be treated."

"Want to be treated—if we were chimps and if our idea of a good time was a handful of oranges."

"Exactly. But we do give them cigarettes, too."

"How the hell is that better?"

"That's what they want. And the vets say one a day doesn't do much statistically to their mortality."

"I suppose they can always leave… oh wait, they can't, can they?"

"True, but at the end of the day, can we?"

"Not yet, your Highness. Not yet!"

They both smiled at this. The shape of the conversation was familiar. Since first meeting many years ago, in dim back rooms amongst funky hippies and bearded eco-terrorists, they had beaten these same ideas back and forth. Things had changed since then. Inheriting economy destabilising amounts of wealth had shifted the game from frustrated impotent bewailing, to empire-building transformation; and, although their methods and principles might differ, the core vision remained locked onto a remote, glittering future they both saw clearly.

"So, you want to take a look at your finished omelette?" said the man.

"Absolutely," replied Niato. "When is *Atlantis On Line* going live?"

"AOL is live. Golden master. You are our first user. When the others get here, we are going to give them the tour and then throw open the doors."

Niato dropped his Spex back down over his eyes and entered the shared space his friend had conjured. The view out to sea and over the forest remained. The sugarcube stacks of stone and the muddy scars had vanished. It was, however, only when he turned his head towards the massive, opencast mine that was Bäna's capital city that the divergence between the AOL's virtual and solid reality became significant.

Atlantis City was a tropical Venice. They had taken liberties with Plato's plans. Instead of concentric canals, they had chosen a single loose spiral, spanned with bridges and lined with delicate, narrow, four or five-storey villas. Tropical jungle infiltrated the city; ferns and palms growing from balconies and terraces, figs and climbers questing out of cracks and chinks between buildings. Lengths of canal bank were left raw with mangrove, or as sandy banks. No people thronged the streets or bridges. The only perceptible movement was from gigantic lizards positioning themselves in the sun, or birds and butterflies fluttering between plants and roofs.

Niato lifted his Spex again. The vision was still a long way from reality. The looping spiral of the Grand Canal was visible, like a tribal scar in the mud, as was the mouth of the colossal pipe, which would link the canal with the ocean and allow clever use of tides to drive a current out from the centre. The basements of the buildings were mostly dug and reinforced. In iceberg fashion, the quaint villas above were mere ornamentation for ten storeys of subterranean living and working space.

With the Spex down again, Niato projected himself into the city and walked some of its alleys and crossed its graceful sandstone bridges.

"Like we said," said the man, "the underground floor-plans are fixed and going in now, but everything above ground can be altered. Once the founding backers are done choosing their pads, we will let in the other players. October is still the official launch, but we'll let some beta-testers in before then."

"I like it."

"I hope so! You designed it!"

"The people are going to design it, and then we will build it."

Like the Caliph's city of Punt, cut into and conglomerated onto the rock of Ras Siyyan, Atlantis City would first live in the virtual before being birthed into atoms. Atlantis On Line, the game they were exploring, commissioned by Niato, was a massive multiplayer pirate-based trading and crafting game. At a nerdier level, it was also a distributed virtual polity. It intersected the real world at the island of Bäna, where the walls between the virtual and real dissolved. Economy, immigration, planning, and hundreds of other aspects of commerce and government would eventually function through the game.

The virtual Atlantis would start as a ghost, but real atoms

and minds would gradually fill out its form.

Successful players, who could afford to buy in-game loot, would own real-world analogues. Of course, the founding backers would be given first dibs. That's what today was about, a virtual real-estate viewing for the billionaire philanthropist early backers. Space and media moguls were fighting for properties along the Atlantis City Grand Canal—real estate, they had been told, which would one day be amongst the most desirable in the solar system.

The novelty of Atlantis, which hovered ambiguously in the media's perceptions between tacky vanity project and ruthless cynical gaming of the world's geo-political rule book, attracted silly amounts of money from across the demographic spectrum.

One night alone, listening to the wind and drowning in the smells of incense and wisteria, Niato had conceived the shape of this plan to honour his grandfather. He hadn't known then how far he would get with this attempt to follow the man's last request and right the family's wrongs.

At first, he hadn't appreciated just how rich his grandfather had made him. He had assumed that, eventually, the money would run out, but slowly he experienced that strange property of money: after reaching some sort of critical mass, it reproduced autonomously. The more he had spent on land and bribes, the more he had accumulated through donations and bequests. When he wanted to build a school or hospital, guilty oligarchs would trip over one another to sponsor museums or libraries.

The revelation he could sell an entire city off plan had kicked the enterprise into a new gear. And karma was rewarding him. His portfolio, especially his tier-one investment in Astrocosmos Near-Earth Mining-Company, continued to deliver torrents of new money. In fact, Niato's wealth was now many times what it had been when he had inherited his grandfather's controlling share in the world's biggest restaurant chain.

Turning towards the dormant volcano, Niato flitted his perception towards the virtual Royal Palace. He let his eyes pierce the rock, tracing the tunnels and rooms driven into its interior, the pipes and heat engines sipping from deep volcanic thermal masses. The tower…

"What do you think?"

"I like it," said Naito. "You've done a great job. There must be a lot of hackers out there that we owe."

"Thanks, I appreciate that. Yeah, there are probably a couple of thousand little nerds typing away as we speak. Most of them would do it for the fun and challenge anyway, but the chance of having an Atlantis passport and a new start! You don't have to worry about owing them. They are loyal to the idea, and to you for building the impossible… and, of course, to their leaders. We are Nebulous!"

Niato suppressed a shiver. He always thought it sounded a little too ominous.

"Don't overdo that stuff. I don't want thousands of your sleeper agents moving in, just to bide their time until you give the signal to overthrow me."

"Ha! Consider it insurance against the temptations of power!"

"Great."

"Oh, by the way, talking about Nebulous," said the man. "We've been helping out a bit with those kidnapped girls you might have read about."

"Oh yes, from my tuna farm?"

"It's not yours. It was your grandfather's. You sold it. But yes. We used some of our BugNet resources to track down the pirates and, funny coincidence, that guy Keith, who we took wingsuiting... Remember him?"

"Sure, the tortured corporate soul... nasty right jab."

"Yeah, that's him. Well, he's just shown up on the radar again. It looks like, after his anti-authoritarian punching spree, he ended up in a UK battlesuit brigade. A few months ago, he got shot up over Zilistan, and something about his story must have been fishy, because he was sent to a high security psychiatric hospital."

"Shit. Poor guy."

"He leads an interesting life. So, then he gets busted out by two talented little hackers we already had our eyes on. They managed to recruit him as the spear for their rescue attempt. Apparently, one or both of them have a thing for one of the girls. We're keeping eyes on it, but it looks like a nicely put together operation. If something goes wrong, we'll send some assets when they get a bit closer."

"Small world," said Niato. "I'm glad he's ended up on the right side. Keep me posted. Let me know how it goes. You know, I don't believe in coincidences. Seems like the universe still has a role to play for Keith Wilson. Maybe we can find some work for him if it turns out okay."

Landed, showered, and checked into another hotel, Keith almost felt like he was on holiday. The kids had given him a day off. The pirates wouldn't be showing up for another couple of days. There had been a lot of briefings and training, but he had spent as much time as he could spare lying naked on the almost unbearably hot sand of a deserted beach, only a few minutes away from his hotel. He kept his new rubber foot on, even when he was naked. It was part of him now. He only took it off to empty sand out of the socket, or at night to let it charge.

The beach was empty, despite being separated from the swarms of tourists on the hotel side by a single tongue of volcanic rock. Keith hadn't considered the possibility that the beach was only deserted because it had a bearded naked man, with a cybernetic foot, lying spreadeagled in the middle of it. He wouldn't have cared, anyway. He was too busy being soothed by white noise from small waves and from the brisk wind rustling through the palms at the top of the beach. The coral sand was white and clean—and, best of all, not soaked in blood or prone to sloughing off clouds of throat-clenching dust. Keith liked to let it run through his fingers.

The day spent surfing and sunbathing seemed to have done more for him than six months in the sterile, tiled whiteness of the army hospital. He didn't even mind the sand. He reckoned the *other* sand must be all gone by now: the seams packed between his buttocks had presumably been washed away by his mysterious Zil saviours, probably by the old hag herself. The grains wedged under his broken nails had lasted longer, and the clumps matted into the filth and scabs of his scalp must have put up a fight. He had shed it slowly. Back in England, he remembered waking up each morning to find a small puddle of the sharp grains in the hollows his hips and shoulders made in the hospital mattress. Possibly, there were still a few specks in his ears or deep under his skin—driven in by shrapnel and left, even after the medics had finished—but he didn't really care about the sand anymore.

Later, he was sipping on a Margarita, while watching the tourists watching the hula dancers. They were mostly the older 'flowery dress and thick plastic jewellery' type. Only a couple of weeks ago, even this excitement would have been too much. He would have been happy then, just staring out of his window, trying to avoid flashbacks of self-mutilating combat suits and bloated piles of rotting peasants...

...nylon dresses, clean and bright against the muted ochre and asparagus shades of once living flesh.

The boys called in the evening, to check he was okay and to go over their plan. Tomorrow, the holiday was over.

***

9 am and he was already up and lying naked on the beach, trying to bake the alcohol and cloudiness from his body. He didn't give his own mental state too much thought, but perhaps he was re-joining society at some level because, today, he had conceded to place a towel over his exposed parts. His Companion showed the pirate ship as it approached. If the boys were right, it would arrive in two more days and, if it followed its usual pattern, it would stop a kilometre out from Port Allen. The pirates would go ashore, and Keith would go sneak aboard to do his one-man ninja commando routine—the kids seemed to have massively overestimated his martial prowess.

At about noon, a beaten-up truck arrived at the little beach where he had been hanging out. A tall, thin, dreadlocked Rasta unfolded himself from the cab.

"Keith Wilson?" The big black man didn't seem bothered or surprised by Keith's nudity. For Keith, sick of the modern flight to Victorian values, this spoke in his favour. He pulled on his shorts and a t-shirt anyway.

"Yeah. You've got a couple of bits for me?"

The guy nodded, and that was it. They unloaded a mostly deflated Zodiac from the back of the Rasta's truck, and then the guy handed Keith a canvas bag containing a revolver and a long parcel wrapped in an oily towel.

"Bolt action."

Keith carefully unwrapped the parcel, squatting down behind the back of the truck for privacy. It was probably thirty years old, but seemed in good condition. His fingers touched it a little too fondly. They were looking forward to stripping and cleaning it later.

Apparently, Joseph the Rasta would be staying to keep an eye on his kit. After they had taken care of business, Keith accepted the joint that was immediately lit and eventually offered. They settled down, spending a pleasant few hours not chatting, waiting for Zaki and Siegfried's packages to arrive.

Just as the sun was starting its descent, Keith's Companion chirped again. He fished it out of his rucksack as they toked on the end of the current joint. On the display, a green triangle ate up the kilometres, closing in on the blue dot that marked their location. Keith, scanning the sky, eventually spotted the green triangle's physical manifestation. Minutes later, the glider was swooping in towards them.

For the first time that day, Joseph showed a trace of emotion, coughing violently with surprise as the giant, silvery blue manta ray glided silently out of the sky and landed next to them on the beach. Keith and Joseph quickly grabbed on to its fins to stop the gentle breeze lifting it away again. On closer inspection, it was less fish and more balloon. Following the boys' prepared instructions, Keith pulled open the beast's belly and dragged out a lightweight nylon bag.

After everything was unpacked, counted, and calibrated, Keith opened a compartment a third of the way down the glider's ventral flank and pulled on a tab to unwind a length of ultra-fine line; attached to the end was a hook apparatus that looked like a lightweight carbon-fibre carabiner. They were instructed to clip the carabiner to something heavy enough to stop it from being dragged away once the

GliderKite caught the wind. They chose one of the metal rings on the cab of the truck that was used to attach its tatty canvas roof.

Without its cargo, the GliderKite seemed almost weightless as they boosted it into the air. The string became taught as the wind and fluid dynamics lifted it vertically into the sky, spooling out string as it rose. Soon, it was a silver glint at the end of 200 metres of ultra-fine line. Then there was an audible click as magnets in the carabiner released, and the string was reeled back up to the body. Unhitched, it was free to start its 12,000 km journey back to the boys. If it was lucky with the wind, it would only take ten days.

They hauled everything onto the back of the truck and drove a couple of kilometres to Joseph's red, gold, and green cabin where, after a glass of rum and another joint, they unpacked the goodies:

- Two tubes linked by a complicated web of wedges and bands. Apparently slaved laser sights and a scope.

- Something like a big black frisbee or small dustbin lid. From a hub in its middle, fan blades projected into the rim and, in the centre, was a tennis ball-sized smoked glass dome. A menacing barrel jutted from its circumference. On what was probably its top, a handwritten note: "Charge me".

- A black spiky snake, as long as Keith's arm, with a fat head. It looked like a giant, evil sperm.

- A black life jacket-shaped piece of clothing made of incredibly thin material and a matching hat.

- 50 cartridges, a pair of rugged-looking Spex and a paint-ball mask.

All of this had been packed into a space the size of three pizza boxes stacked on top of one another.

The nice pair of military Spex and the cartridges would come in handy; the other items were less obvious. Some bits were reminiscent of some of the better tech thrown against them, while they tried to integrate the many jingoistic pockets of hatred that had seemed to stretch from Biarritz to Ulan Bator.

Faced with all these fascinating and clearly highly illegal toys, Joseph was having trouble staying cool. The boys, amazingly perceptive considering they were half a world away, noticed his interest while they chatted and utilised his enthusiasm. His first task was to fill the black stealth life jacket with sand. On the face of it, a puzzling request, until, in a flash, Keith realised it was not a life jacket, but a bulletproof vest—bring your own ballast style. "Just in case," the boys assured him.

While Joseph was filling the vest's laminar pockets, Keith took the sights and let Zaki walk him through their assembly: he used the supplied clamps and rubber wedges to attach one tube, the laser sight apparently, underneath the rifle's barrel, then the more familiar scope to the rails on top. They spent the next forty minutes calibrating, turning screws by half turns, and every now and then letting the tech run through self-test cycles. Finally, in a chirpy synthetic voice, it asked Keith to fire a few shots at a distant tree.

Like guns Keith had used before, the laser and the scope could both automatically adjust themselves. The scope, packed full of image recognition software, could be told to keep a target centred, compensating for minor wobbles like a good camera image stabilisation system. A little nipple-like joystick, aligned comfortably for thumb operation, guided the laser over the scope's rock-solid target. Once selected, the laser would illuminate that spot and, once the trigger was squeezed, the gun would wait for the best moment to fire. Smart bullets with their tiny fins would do their best to correct drift, the laser on the barrel lighting up the target until the bullets had found their mark.

Joseph plugged a little compressor into his truck and inflated the Zodiac. Then, together, they dragged it down the beach to just above a line of seaweed and storm debris. Joseph mounted the outboard and hinged it out the way to be ready when needed.

The unpacking and setup had taken the rest of the afternoon and half of the evening. Keith was starving, but Zaki and Segi badgered him into a few more hours of work. They had written a simulation of the pirate boat and programmed in their attack plans and the various failover contingencies for each. That night and the next day would be spent dry-running the assault. Keith would run around in a Spex-generated virtual environment. Joseph would babysit him in the real world in case someone stumbled across him and became spooked by a sunburnt white man running around with a gun. They had a prepared excuse:

'It's okay, it's not loaded. He's having a bad trip. He'll be fine in a couple of hours.'

***

02:00 - Keith, suited up in his bulletproof vest with the Remington in a water-tight bag slung over his shoulders, wades into the warm sea with an inflatable tube that will, hopefully, prevent the sand-filled hat and vest from dragging him to the bottom—the vest has a quick release to be used in the event of drowning. He expected Joseph to ferry him out to the boat for his suicide mission, but apparently the boys have a 'better' idea.

02:45 - A still stunned Keith is making good progress through the gentle swell, pulled along behind a dolphin, who claims to be a citizen of the Kingdom of Atlantis. The dolphin is wearing its own bulletproof jacket and some kind of gimp-mask muzzle with a ridge running from the tip of its nose to just behind its blow hole. It has apparently been following the pirates for days, and is very grateful when Keith is able to readjust the vest and rub petroleum jelly on its pressure sores.

03:50 - They have arrived at the boat. Less than a hundred metres away, through the scope, Keith can clearly see two guys on watch. One looks like an extra from a pirate film with a fetching scar, eyepatch, and scruffy ponytail. He is ambling around with an Uzi. The second, who would not look out of place in any mundane urban setting with his chubby jowls and potbelly, is on the bridge, alternately looking at something that illuminates his face with a green cast and staring out of the windows. Apparently, there are three more pirates asleep down below, including the captain.

04:35 - The pirates returning from shore leave are getting ready to embark at Port Allen. Crystal clear, real-time images, apparently relayed from a friendly seagull—Keith has stopped being incredulous by this point—show the jovial pirates casting off. The one they have identified as Pedro, the owner of the DNA found in the decoy junk, and also at the scene of the bar room murder in Papua New Guinea, sits at the prow of the little boat.

04:40 - The dolphin has gone off to plant comms relays on the hull of the pirate ship. Keith floats around, feeling vulnerable; then, when he is told to, he lets the evil sperm into the water, where it swims away.

04:47 - The snake bot ascends an anchor chain. On deck, it opens its mouth and allows its passenger to crawl out. The chipped cockroach, which has been sitting on a damp, sugar-soaked wad of cotton wool for the past two weeks, reorients itself and then heads across the boat's deck and through an open window.

05:09 - The dolphin leaves, heading in the direction of the returning revellers.

05:10 - The cockroach has found the room with the girls. The location is tagged on all their maps. Everything is going as planned; they are still on scenario A1.

05:18 – Pedro and the rest of the returning pirates are still 25 minutes away. Keith, being super careful not to get the rifle wet, sights on the Uzi-toting pirate's arse. Hardly needing all the advanced tech at this range, he fires. The pirate feels a sharp pain in his left buttock and sticks his hand down his shorts to scratch the buried sliver of glass he assumes is an insect bite.

05:25 - After trying for five minutes to get a clean shot through *the window to put another micro-flechette into the other pirate, Keith gives up. They switch to plan A3.*

05:40 - The cockroach is now in position A3: crouching on the bedside table of the pirate captain, providing real-time telemetry. Siegfried is flying their dustbin lid drone, keeping it hovering 200m above the boat.

05:41 - Zaki drops two penetrators from the high-altitude GliderKites. The guided tungsten darts begin their 20,000m descent.

05:42 - Siegfried's drone drops from the sky, tilts through a half-open door, powers down a passageway, then does an elegant aerial flip before using its magnets to attach itself to the ceiling.

The crewman on the bridge turns; he may have heard something. On command, Keith shoots a conventional bullet through his head. Simultaneously, Zaki remotely detonates the poison-filled micro-flechette, nestling in the buttock of the first pirate. A short time later, he is an ex-pirate, dead, deceased, run down the curtain, and gone to join the 'choir invisible'.

Seconds later, the two 10kg tungsten penetrator darts slam into, then through, the ship travelling at nearly 500mph. One smashes through two decks and annihilates the ship's engine in a massive transfer of kinetic energy; the other, lacking anything solid to collide with, punches through the roof of the captain's cabin, detonates its explosive charge, and continues on as a cloud of supersonic shrapnel through the deck below, after incidentally turning the pirate captain into a cloud of vaporised flesh and blood.

05:43 - Finally waking up, the remaining two pirates stagger out of their bunks. Taking control of the drone hanging from the ceiling outside their cabin, Zaki shoots them, one after the other, with the drone's stubby 9mm cannon.

2km away, the returning pirates see the fireball from the engine rise silently into the night. They begin shouting and pulling out guns. However, their enthusiasm is cut off when a vicious spike turns the bottom of their small wooden boat into a colander. With wild shooting and considerable panic, the boat quickly sinks, dragged under by its heavy outboard motor.

At 06:08, the last of the drowning pirates is systematically stabbed to death by a vengeful dolphin, wearing a diamond-tipped spike on its nose, narwhal-style.

***

Keith floated in the warm sea until he got the all-clear from his controllers and then paddled over to the Long Liner. After a new message—they were not 100% sure, but it might be sinking faster than expected—he ditched his sand-filled hat and jacket and increased his pace. After he clambered aboard, stepping over the dead pirate sprawled on deck, he headed below to where the Spex were telling him the girls were being held. Another body was washing back and forth along the short corridor in the ten centimetres of bloody water that was, as he watched, creeping up the sides of the walls. The last door was locked with a bicycle chain looped through heavy brass eyes nailed to the door and frame.

"Get back!" he shouted. "The boat's sinking. I'm going to get you out!"

He booted the door a couple of times until it flew open. Red-stained water poured in, carrying the body with it. A girl screamed, but several began shouting and stamping on the back of the deceased pirate, sending waves of water splashing around the small room. The space was packed with about thirty terrified Asian females. He scanned around and recognised Stella from the pictures the boys had sent him. As his gaze found her, a huge cheer rose up from whoever else was tele-present at the other end of the video feed his Spex were transmitting. He recognised Zaki and Segi's voices, but there now seemed to be many more. The tricky part of the operation was over; the viewers on the other end had been un-muted.

"Come on, he's dead. Let's go. The ship is sinking!"

Keith turned and stepped back into the corridor, waving for the girls to exit post-haste. One was not finished with her stamping; she had fallen onto her knees to beat the back of the dead man's head with her fists. Keith had to drag her out through the knee-deep water.

They joined the rest of the party on the deck, where panic was reigning. Some of the girls were already clambering down towards the Zodiac that Joseph had pulled alongside, but they would not all fit. For the first time, things were not going as planned, and it was looking nasty. The Long Liner was sinking startlingly quickly. When the engine blew, it must have blasted a vast hole in the hull. The girls had started screaming again, but Keith noticed Stella dive elegantly into the water, her inertia carrying her away from any dangerous undertow. Following her lead, the others also plunged into the oily water. Most seemed to understand from Keith and Joseph's arm-flailing that they should get away from the sinking vessel.

With a huge sound of rending metal and bubbling, the prow thrust fifteen metres up into the air and then began to slide quickly out of view beneath the waves.

The situation had deteriorated rapidly. Keith was in the water again. He couldn't count the bobbing heads in the dark, but he could hear a lot of screams for help. Suddenly, he was aware of something large in the water with him. Flashes of frenzied shark death presented themselves for his inner eye's perusal. He recoiled, jarred away from merely imaginary horrors when a vicious 60cm knife—which seemed fouled with gore—thrust up through the waves a metre or so away.

"Take off his fucking spike, it's got stuck!" screeched a voice through the buds of his Spex. Keith got the impression it had been shouting at him for a while.

The blade, which had hinged forward to provide a handy stabbing tool, had become wound with pirate clothing and jammed. Keith found that he had to peel off the entire neoprene mask to get rid of the gruesome weapon. He jerked back to avoid its blade as it sank safely away.

The water was warm and, once the girls realised it was a dolphin with good intentions, rather than a ravenous shark, that was circling them, things calmed down. Joseph and twelve girls were in the little inflatable, while Keith, Stella, and the rest held onto ropes with exhausted arms.

Nobody seemed to be missing. Tinkerbell had helped the less proficient swimmers to the Zodiac and was now nuzzling at Stella's side. The coastguard was on the way.

It looked like they had done it. Media streams had already started picking up their public feeds.

Energy cannot be created or destroyed. The First Law of Thermodynamics is unambiguous.

Electrical potential created in the spinning coils of a coal-fuelled power station is a withdrawal of chemical energy originally deposited by sunlight millions of years ago: an auditable chain of transmutation, from solar photons, to plant carbohydrates, to mineralised coal, then to heat, angular momentum and, finally, into the electrical potential used to power your fridge.

A nuclear power station does the same thing by liquidating a longer-term investment. This ancient energy, required to build the massive nuclei of radioactive elements, was laid down by supernovae firing hundreds of millions of years before our planet was even formed.

The universe is rife with energy. Generation is not the problem: solar, wind, tide, thermal, nuclear. There are, however, few means to store it as conveniently as in fossil fuels.

It takes 250 calories—one megajoule—to accelerate a car to 100mph. This is about the same amount of chemical energy as stored in one shot glass of petrol. The energy is liberated by burning the fuel in air, and the waste products blown back into the same gaseous waste bin for someone else to worry about. To generate the same energy, an electric car needs 1kg of charged batteries and a lot of other expensive and complicated components.

Nuclear fuel can hold millions of times as much energy

in the same volume. A hypothetical nuclear-powered auto would only burn a grain of salt's worth of fuel to drive around all day. In practice, however, nuclear engines tend to be dangerous and dirty. Even if they could be miniaturised, nobody wants a billion little autonomous nuclear reactors creeping through their cities or buzzing through their skies.

It seems that some technologies just don't want to die. Despite the awareness of the indignities that fossil fuels foist on the environment, after two hundred years of looking for alternatives, they are still the energy storage medium of choice for far too many scenarios.

Professor Dominic Griffin clamped the sample and closed the leaded glass hatch. He screwed the butterfly nuts to seal the chamber and tested the vacuum. Then he withdrew to the bench, where he began powering up the accelerator.

The tiny Hafnium target, a purple and blue marble, was magnified in one window of a blackboard-sized panel. The professor would shortly begin the proton bombardment, pumping in energy from the hulking cyclotron in the next room.

The ball of protons and neutrons that make up an atom's nucleus, deforms and wobbles like a fat lady's bum when struck by the slap of an incoming high-energy proton. Hafnium was unique in that if spanked just right; its nucleus would flip into a new shape—imagine clenched buttocks— and could hold this metastable nuclear configuration for years. Eventually, and randomly, it would relax back to its original, unclenched form, releasing a blast of gamma energy in the process.

The breakthrough that Griffin and his grad students had made, and now were tweaking, was to coax the primed Hafnium to release its stored energy on demand. Although thousands of times less energetic than a true nuclear reaction, it could be used as a fuel source with thousands of times the energy density of the best chemical alternatives.

It would change the world.

***

Except it wouldn't. Not if Niato's small, but highly-trained, team of hackers and critters had anything to do with it.

He felt sorry for the guy. The camera angle, from cockroach height above the floor, was hardly optimal, but he could clearly sense the excitement in the man's body language.

The research was highly restricted, and nobody had tried yet to reproduce the experiments. One day, undoubtedly, they would and then they would find that the papers contained nothing but a gibberish of ludicrous parameters and flawed theoretical work.

The servers and instruments in the lab had been so thoroughly compromised that, since the start of the project, every formula and calculation had been corrupted. Systematic errors had been introduced at every stage in the research, from the initial fundamental literature review to the custom simulation of nuclear decay. As a final twist of the knife, the research papers had been peppered with subtle math typos and silly schoolboy errors to make the scientists look like amateurs.

The hack's finesse was that, despite the garbling of information, the experiments worked. Real science had been done. Malicious perversion of parameters and equations in the research were symmetrically unscrambled by the equally hacked experimental equipment. The only people who knew the real values and formulae were Niato and his cohort of Nebulous hackers.

Griffin would be ridiculed. If enough shit could be thrown at him, the whole field might be mothballed for decades.

It was a horrible thing to do to a perfectly good scientist. Had Niato thought for a second that the technology might truly eliminate fossil fuels, or genuinely improve life, he wouldn't have got involved. Unfortunately, Hafnium nuclei, once packed full of energy, could be forced to release this payload in a single nasty burst. A blast, a thousand times more powerful than the best plastique, would be destructive enough on its own. But, considerably more destabilising to a world that already had enough ways to re-format the biosphere, was the reaction's potential to trigger direct nuclear fusion without having to mess around with critical mass quantities of fissile material.

Nuclear warheads as small as cigars were not a cosy prospect.

"When is the presentation?"

"Three weeks."

Niato nodded and watched Griffin fiddling with the settings. "Poor chap, he has no idea what is about to hit him."

"As it should be."

"And we are going in tomorrow?"

"No, Sir, Sunday."

"Okay, yes, I remember. The BBQ. Less chance that some-body will be working at the weekend."

"Exactly."

"Right, then proceed. You have my final approval."

"Yes, Sir!"

The Commander snapped a salute and turned to go. Niato looked at the screen again. Then, as he heard the click of the opening door, he called the officer back.

"Wait. Last-minute change. The man from the rescue of the girls… you know who I mean?"

"Yes, Sir," said the Commander, turning back from the door.

"I want him brought into the mission."

"What?!" the man blurted, then recovered something of his composure and continued. "Your Highness, we've been planning this operation for nearly two years. It is simply impossible to add another team member at this stage!"

"Commander, the universe works in mysterious ways. I

have a feeling he is meant to be part of this."

The King could be frustrating to a rational military mind. *Too much time meditating with monks or munching mushrooms,* the enlisted men joked. The officers, fiercely loyal to their king, wouldn't tolerate such subversive mutterings amongst the men; in private, however, they would also grumble light-heartedly about their ruler's penchant for esoteric mumbo jumbo.

"Sir, there are a lot of specialist skills that cannot be trained in an afternoon…"

"Did you watch the feeds? Have you read his backstory? And as for special skills, I trained him myself, back when you were still shooting civilians on the Kashmir border."

The Commander winced as if struck. Like many in the Atlantean navy, his previous military history had been a journey of guilt and shame, marbled with veins of heroism and distinguished service. He had joined the Hind army as little more than a boy, nearly twenty years ago, full of hope and a naive belief in his people. What he had seen and been made to do in the years that followed had worn his soul down to a nub. The King had recruited him and many others, head-hunted them from the world's armies and police forces, spoken of the necessity and rightfulness of the warrior's way. Given them a just cause.

"Sorry, Your Highness. I will see what can be done."

The airport's boards were looping re-runs: cavorting dolphin antics, Keith waving to a group of girls as they climbed the steps, all dressed in white, bedecked with garish garlands. A sanitised upbeat outro to the media show now spinning down.

Keith turned away from a screen attached to a supporting pillar and looked out of a physical window instead. A plane was climbing into the orange evening.

Aboard the flight back to Manila, the girls would enjoy hero status in First Class, filmed and live-streamed, sipping their sparkling wine and eating caviar. Disembarking, they would head to immigration, while the reporters headed for connecting flights. Within twenty-four hours, the news would have moved on, and most of the rescued victims would be back in their old grubby lives, many in the same brothels they had been kidnapped from.

Keith stood next to Joseph. Both wore newly gifted khaki shorts and shirts, props from the networks. When the last shots were in the bag, tiny camera drones had dropped and folded themselves snuggly into the carry cases of young, scruffy tech interns. A couple of the immaculately dressed, severe yet beautiful anchors came over to shake hands and say goodbye. The adrenalin-fuelled whirlwind was over. The circus was packing up and moving on.

Joseph felt it, too. He shrugged and stuck out his arm to Keith. "Walk good, bro."

Keith took the wiry, calloused hand and shook it firmly. "Stay safe. We should do it again some time!"

Joseph looked at him sceptically, and then the ageing Rasta turned away into the crowd. Keith watched the red, black, and green knitted hat as it cut a line through the purple, orange, and turquoise tourist throng.

Keith was alone. Free and aimless for the first time since limited options had nudged him into the army, four and a half years before. The reporters had all gone; the girls were safe. Joseph would be outside in the sun by now, halfway through a crumpled joint. Staring out of the window and pondering his options, Keith decided 'free' probably did not fully describe his situation.

He was AWOL. The media had described his daring one-man escape from the military hospital, where he had been recovering from post-traumatic stress, aggravated by traumatic loss of a foot. He was a fugitive. Equal measures of hero and household name, but also persona non grata across much of the world. While the blaze of public adoration still warmed his skin he would be protected, but the media was already turning away its gaze, and His Majesty's government was much less fickle. They would not be forgetting his infraction any time soon, or giving up their option to use his body as a tool for dealing violence—Keith the biological bludgeon.

He had no intention of returning to the army. Even the thought brought back the sweats and a rising panic.

He stood near the windows looking out. The Manila flight was long gone. Another plane must have been delayed, because all around him Nipponese travellers were arriving and sitting down on the polished concrete. He began to feel uncomfortable, as if he was intruding on a private party. He moved off. Walking without goal or destination.

Inevitably, he ended up in a bar. Ironically, an English-themed place, called the Big Ben. At the next table, a lady recognised him, and Keith heard her pointing him out to her friend. She had probably been learning yoga or limbo dancing or something for the past week and was now heading home to work the year's fifty-one remaining weeks, dreaming the whole time of her next exotic soiree. Keith sipped on his Bloody Mary, savouring the vodka fumes that lifted off its surface.

"Hi," the woman said nervously. "You're the man from the TV who rescued those poor girls, aren't you?"

Keith wasn't sure how to react to these approaches. Once or twice, he had swung too far to the sarcastic end of the spectrum, prompting unexpectedly severe responses. Apparently, people were entitled to his time, now that he shone from their screens. In the other direction, when he had been too earnest and open, getting rid of his clingy new 'friends' had taken effort. So he went with a neutral:

"Hi, yes, I am."

"That's so brave!"

"Thanks, but I was just doing my job," he lied.

"So, a big hero's welcome waiting and lots of pretty ladies making a fuss over you back home, I guess?"

Publicly, GOV.UK was commending him on his bravery,

spamming hints they had been behind the operation, while avoiding all mention of his breakout. Their SpinBot Sages had done such a good job, it was difficult for Keith to watch the news reports and backstory features without feeling a patriotic swell.

In private communications, the tone was different, threatening him with everything from prison to publicity tours as an UK MOD recruitment tool. He was sure that, if he went home, he would get a very public hero's welcome, followed by a very private debriefing. If they could not convince him to turn shill, this would be quickly followed by rendition and indefinite detention.

"Maybe," he replied to his new fan, playing these future scenarios over in his mind.

"Well, you should. You deserve it!"

"Thanks," Keith smiled and turned back to his drink, hoping to end the conversation on a high point.

The lady and her friend continued to glance at him from time to time as they whispered to each other. He drained his drink. During the consumption of a second, he rolled around the idea of 'reaching out' to his old employer. He was sure that, in light of recent changes to his status, BHJ would be willing to overlook some of the past silliness and make a place in their organisation for an ex-soldier and war hero. Ben might be pissed off, but that was actually a point in the idea's favour. Keith fished out the fancy Spex the boys had given him and started composing a message to George, Ben's father.

He was slightly drunk by now and his brainwaves were obviously a little confused because, although he was focusing on subvocalising a polite professional job application, some form of technologically enhanced Tourette's kept interspersing foul and sexually explicit slurs throughout the text. By the fourth drink, the ladies were long gone, having made their goodbyes, and posed for their selfies. Keith's application letter had turned into a rambling confused rant. Expending his last reserves of sobriety and good judgement, he deleted it and disgustedly stuck the Spex back in his rucksack.

Keith was painfully aware how fleeting his current fame was likely to be. He also knew that, however ephemeral this celebrity, drunk, alone in an airport lounge, surrounded by hundreds of citizen snaparazzi, he would have to stay sharp or be cast as another celebrity meltdown and next minute's snack-able mass titillation. He pulled down his baseball cap, but left off his shades. It was a tightrope walk: he didn't want to be recognised—snapped and live-streamed, stumbling over a pram or coming out of the lady's toilet—but equally, he didn't want to look too suspicious and get shot or bundled into a room to be fondled intimately by men with rubber gloves. He dug around for the Spex again and slid them over his eyes as an additional barrier against the world. A message was waiting.

```
*** A Hero's welcome ***
Congratulations Keith Wilson @keithWils0n4! You have
won #RitzzWorldHero of the week!
This week's Ritzz Cigarette prize is a free all-inclusive
holiday at the Cancun Blue Bay Hotel Mexico!

WOW! Two weeks all expenses paid with First Class flight
and Five Star food and accommodation!

Each week, Ritzz and our loyal Branditos and Brandinos
select an outstanding individual, who has gone beyond
```

```
the call of duty to make a difference.
#Change the @World! Smoke @Ritzz!

This offer expires in 19 minutes 36 seconds.
HNL -> IAH:IAH -> CUN Flight AN767 21:40

<<Accept and Confirm>>
```

Keith was ready instantly to bin the message, wondering how this blatant spam had blasted through the industrial-strength filters he had put up to block the recent barrage of media and fanboy attention, but something snagged in his mind. Info screens, wrapping a three-metre-tall replica of Big Ben, were cycling through lewd marketing, passenger information, and departure times. He was looking as the flight times appeared again, and it was there: Honolulu to George Bush International, nine-forty. The gate would be announced in twenty minutes.

A holiday would be nice, he allowed himself to think. It would give him time to get his head together and decide what to do next. Yet, simultaneously, he was asking himself how hopeless his life had become that junk mail might hold the answer. He spawned his own MiniSage and allocated it a few fractions of a Coin before sending it off to check the certificates and do basic forensics.

Two empty glasses still sat on the table in front of him, with a screwed-up napkin and a shredded cardboard beer mat. He had 'left' the hospital sixteen days ago, wearing nothing but military asylum pyjamas. His worldly goods were utterly meagre and mostly in his backpack. At the hotel were some clothes and snorkelling gear; everything else was with him. Anyway, apart from his passport and some money, his only real possession of any value was attached securely to his ankle stump.

The Sage came back, green and smiling. Keith evaluated his options. The board flicked to the flights again. Still eighteen minutes. The waitress was busy, so he conjured up one of the restaurant's avatars with his Spex. A ridiculous parody of a busty barmaid appeared from some fictional back room and bounced over. In a grotesque approximation of a cockney accent, *she* greeted him and dropped into a scripted sales patter. Keith couldn't be bothered to listen; he only had seventeen minutes, so he interrupted and brusquely ordered a Chicken Kiev and another drink.

The Bloody Mary arrived, carried by a surly youth, who made a vague pretence at tidying away the crap that covered Keith's table. Preoccupied, Keith pulled out the little umbrella from his drink and flicked it away across the debris-strewn table. The kid watched the drops of drink spray across the surface and the umbrella tumble onto the floor. He then shrugged, put the glasses back down, and dropped the handful of napkins and mat fragments. He also dropped his cloth and pointedly didn't wipe up the new tomato splatter. Keith reminded himself to try and treat humans better.

Ignoring the finger actually squashing one of his French fries, he attempted a smile when the kid returned with his blackened orange lozenge a few minutes later. The gate was now up. The plane was boarding. Keith flicked the maimed chip off his plate. It landed in the little pool of red liquid.

A smartly dressed woman apologised and squeezed behind Keith's chair, aiming for the free table next to him. She hesitated as she took in the mess of spilt drinks and miscellaneous detritus piled up in front of Keith. She looked around for an alternative, but the restaurant was full. Displaying unambiguous signs of revulsion, the lady slid into the seat and pulled out her Companion. Keith let his eyes linger. There was no danger of making eye contact. Her body language made it clear that he didn't exist in her universe.

He cut into his Kiev, fork pressing into the crust and beginning to penetrate the chicken pressure hull. Inside, the cavity was filled with a mix of superheated molten garlic butter and compressed steam. In slow motion, the fork's metal spikes broke the integrity of the Kiev capsule. Pressure dropped explosively as gas and liquid rushed out of the puncture. With the pressure drop, the remaining fluid was free to boil and generate more of the scolding pyroclastic aerosol of garlic butter.

Some small sound caused her to turn. The scruffy man was momentarily obscured by a mini explosion. He yelped and rocked back on his chair, attempting to escape the apparently very hot stream of something vile that issued from his nasty burnt tube of processed grease. A few small drops of garlic fat landed on her Companion, solidifying instantly on contact with the cool glass. She wiped the grease off with a tissue and went back to ignoring him, while she waited for her salad and tea.

"Fuck! Fuck! Shit!" then "Whoa, arrgg, FUCK!" shouted Keith as the butter, like the venom spat from a furious snake, penetrated his still closing eyes. The pain subsided momentarily and Keith found that, with his spasm of recoil, he had tipped his chair onto the cusp of a topple. He briefly made eye contact with the woman. Then, gravity seemed to cough politely and, despite a good attempt at a flailing recovery, the chair continued its arc and slow motion crash to the ground.

Swearing constantly, Keith disentangled himself from the chair and wiped with his hands at his greasy, burning face. The surly teenage waiter and half of the restaurant looked on with either horror or mirth. Many had devices pointed at him. He was probably already trending.

The Kiev was gone. At some point, during the previous few seconds of excitement, it must have rolled from the plate and joined him on the floor. He wanted to continue shouting obscenities, or at least berate the staff for their ridiculous lethal food, but he had already provided enough of a spectacle. He grabbed his stuff, slapped a five hundred note on the table, and turned to stride stoically out of shot—

Passengers streamed by on their way to the gates. They waved their Companions or virtual cards at him as they passed. The gate steward inspected each, his Spex adding metadata, giving him a second for each to reach his own conclusions, before passing on its expert system evaluation. It had been a long day. He let a small queue form as he allowed himself to be distracted by the hilarious slapstick routine playing out in the Big Ben bar.

—but the epic battle was not over. The wounded Kiev, still oozing its green speckled pus, lodged itself under Keith's heel. Amply lubricated, the crusty pad slid across the ersatz wood and carried Keith to the ground once more.

To the surprise of the young couple pushing their sleeping infant and attempting to get his attention, the gate steward let out a spluttering chortle. He continued to ignore them while watching the limping, buttery bloke as he shambled forwards. The guy was a complete fuck-up, his face a dangerous crimson, as he staggered closer. He was making very poor progress. The man was clearly drunk. Then, in horror, the steward realised there was something else—the man's foot was pointing the wrong way! The gate steward now contemplated the possibility that he was dealing with an outbreak of shambling zombiism. Whatever was up, this was way outside normal passenger behaviour. As the man approached, the steward reached his hand to his lapel to call additional security. The thing that was realistically, probably not a zombie, crossed the remaining ground and arrived emitting a garlicky smog. It fumbled with its Companion and looked desperately at the steward.

Keith was aware that people were stopping and watching his painful progress toward the departures arch, where a man in a flight attendant's uniform stood prepping himself for what looked to be an inevitable showdown. Rubber foot flapping, they drew level. Keith waved what he hoped was a boarding pass and not a spam Trojan phishing lure. The certificate and encrypted data jumped visibly across to the steward's Spex in the form of a black domino, surrounded by a swarm of churning metadata.

Blank confusion, followed by a slack-jawed stare of incredulity, registered on the steward's face. He then took half a step backward.

"Enjoy your flight, Sir. And Sir, sorry, the other way. It's the left-hand arch for First Class."

Keith continued his shamble in slightly better spirits, promising himself that he would use the two weeks in Mexico to sort out his life.

Having taken time to twist his foot, so it is pointing in the right direction, Keith is hustling to the plane. His name had been called privately and politely via his Spex, then publicly and impatiently over the airport PA. The gate corridor is empty; everybody must already be on board. He curses and breaks into a jog. The corridor twists, and he sees the aircraft door is open, which is a good sign. The stewardess is also still smiling as he boards. He apologises to her profusely.

"Not a problem at all, Mr Wilson. This way, please."

He is shown to his First Class capsule cabin. On the way, Keith glances down the fuselage, past the curtain that separates the First Class Roomettes from rows of bulky Business Class seats. Further back, beyond a second curtain, more seats are packed even closer—knee room a cruel memory. Over the last few years, Keith has flown thousands of kilometres on a shaking roaring tiltrotor, so he has little pity for travellers in coach class. The flight seems to have a lot of empty seats.

The pod door is a feather membrane that he pushes through like a bead curtain. It seals itself after him; the beads seeking partners and magnetically binding. Discontinuities and flaws from the chaotic annealing process work themselves to the edges, or seek complementary pairs to cancel out. It is so fascinating to watch that Keith pushes his hand roughly through the curtain again, just to watch the process a second time.

He settles into his 'seat', which is a complicated piece of

machinery so responsive and eager to please that, as it adjusts to his rump and moves beneath his trapezius, he drops momentarily into an unpleasant flashback of being back in his battlesuit.

Another stewardess arrives with drinks. The feather membrane parts automatically to let her lean through with a tray. Keith leaves the champagne and takes an orange juice.

'Time to get straight,' he thinks, looking out of the oversized window. He settles back and the plane begins to taxi.

A big, illuminated sign slides by on the airport terminal roof.

"Aloha," he mumbles back to it. "What a week!"

Time to relax and get things sorted out in his head. On the plus side, he has earned significant reputation-credit with the Silicium Clan, and the anonymous Coins transferred to his wallet will keep him in medium-quality accommodation for a couple of months, at least. He is also famous. He winces and lets his Spex run the trending video of him flapping around on the restaurant floor like a wounded pigeon. Spam filters are straining as he is offered dozens of product placements and marketing gigs. The Mesh is loving his disarming combination of action hero and buffoon.

The plane picks up speed. Keith lets his eyes close and allows the rumbling acceleration to carry him back into the padding of his seat.

When he wakes, it is dark outside. Looking backwards out

of the window, he watches the wing tip light blinking to itself. Distant thunderheads are illuminated from beneath with moonlight. As he surfaces back to wakefulness, he becomes aware that his bladder is signalling urgently that it requires relief.

Corridor lights are dimmed, but in the gloom he notices the many empty seats stepping off into the darkness. There don't seem to be any stewardesses around, either. It's all a bit spooky, dark and still against the dull roar of the engines. Way down at the back of the plane, there is light and movement. Keith ignores another toilet—curiosity beating the outraged petitions of his bladder—and continues towards the signs of life. He passes a stewardess coming the other way, pushing a trolley in the parallel lane. She is apparently serving oddly sized portions of something to the empty seats.

At the back of the plane, a number of passengers are incongruously getting changed in the aisle. They are standing around in sporty looking Lycra underwear, seemingly comfortable in their partial nudity. A big, muscular chap is handing out duty free bags from an overhead locker. The others take the bags and pull out the contents.

There is more action taking place in the aft galley. As the curtain twitches, Keith hears snippets of conversation as he approaches.

"…keep it tight and it won't flap…"

"That should give you six minutes…"

When they notice him, they stop and turn, watching him

silently as he closes the remaining few metres. They are all fit, in a lean functional way, but one particular rear profile strikes him as a fine model of a human being. She is familiar, but even as she turns towards him and their eyes meet, he can't place her.

"Hi, Keith. I hope you are enjoying the flight."

"Dee! Bloody hell, what are you doing here?"

"Same as you, I would imagine."

"What?" Keith is befuddled. "You won a holiday? What, all of you?" He realises how implausible this sounds, even as he is suggesting it. "Why are you standing there in your pants?"

There is murmuring and chuckling from the others.

"A holiday, is that what you think? Then I probably have some bad news for you," Dee says, looking genuinely troubled.

***

The stewardess has finished dealing out her packages and returns the trolley to the bulkhead. Various-sized bundles, wrapped in an eclectic mix of cloth napkins, now rest on many of the seats.

A pair of the black-clad figures are making their way towards the front of the plane. They are carrying multiple plastic spray bottles hung around their necks. Every couple of rows, one will stop, select a bottle, and spray a few squirts of the contents onto a seat or armrest. The fluid is a familiar dark red.

From the front of the plane, there is a shout and the others quickly sit down and strap themselves in. Keith looks at Dee, and she nods towards an empty seat across the aisle from her.

"What's going on…" Keith starts to say, as two colossal concussions turn the tube of the plane into a massive, badly tuned musical instrument. For an indeterminate amount of time, they are shaken and tumbled. Keith is pulled around in his seat, straining against his seatbelt, while grabbing onto the headrest in front for dear life. The experience is similar to being in a violent and sadistic roller coaster, but without the intellectual assurance that it will all be okay.

The team had obviously been expecting something, because there is little unsecured debris flying around. Packages and 'napkins' have become separated. A severed arm is lying on Keith's lap when the plane finally restores itself to level flight. He shrugs the arm away, and it slips to the floor, leaving a black shiny stain on his Kevlar and Lycra trousers. Although he has seen far worse over the years, he is still shaken by this sudden and intimate horror, also by the fact that the plane seems to be in a very steep dive and experiencing a worrying amount of turbulence. Some drastic and un-aerodynamic modification seems to have been brutally applied to the fuselage.

It is impossible to speak, so Dee takes Keith's hand and leads him towards the front of the plane. She nudges him into a First Class pod. As the membrane curtain shuts behind them, the pod's sonic insulation moderates some of the intolerable screech. They lounge awkwardly on the fully reclined bed/chair. The necessity of proximity forces Dee's Lycra-coddled thigh to press against Keith's suddenly hypersensitive leg. It is inappropriately intimate. Instincts and parasympathetic reflexes misjudge the situation and reroute circulation accordingly. A twinge against runkled fabric reminds Keith that he still badly needs to visit the lav.

Dee doesn't seem to notice his discomfort; she seems to be counting off something in her head. She looks up a fraction of a second before another explosion arrives, with more horrific squealing of tortured metal. Keith's ears pop uncomfortably, and the feather membrane bulges outward.

The King doesn't believe in coincidences, Dee explains.

"He is also pretty serious about his Buddhism," she continues.

Keith learnt that, to the King, the universe is a sea of karma, and it was inconceivable that Keith—a combat-hardened hero with real hands-on experience of WingSuit flying—arrived on the metaphorical radar at the same time the King was pulling the trigger on this mission years in the planning.

It was something more than chance; it was fate reaching down and touching their lives.

It was a sign.

The others get up and start doing lots of complicated things calmly and efficiently; there is no sense of panic. It is all quite surreal. Keith recognises the practised automatic movements that come from hours of training.

The sound steps down through a succession of screaming harmonics; octaves of noise arrive, first as a screeching whine that makes the eyes hurt, before leaving the sensorium at the other end of the audio spectrum as a pounding felt through chest and feet, rather than heard with the ears.

Keith had protested to Dee. He didn't like the idea of becoming a mascot and had refused to have anything to do with whatever it was they were suggesting. Dee had then apologetically informed Keith that options were limited. Unfortunately, the plane had recently flown through a flock of migrating birds. DNA analysis would later identify them as Canada Geese. She elaborated this fact as if there was any chance he was interested. The birds had passed through both port engines, doing terrible damage on the way. Unable to safely shut down the engines, one turbine would explode, piercing the cabin. The plane would descend in an attempt to survive the rapid depressurisation. It would limp on in a desperate attempt to land, but begin to lose integrity, eventually crashing into a nondescript concrete and glass building, somewhere in the under-populated Texas interior.

Keith was welcome to stay on board. His presence would even contribute to the success of the mission by adding one more decoy-mangled human body, but they had already distributed enough bits and pieces of human chaff around the cabin to fool DNA analysis. They didn't really need any more help creating the illusion that the plane had been packed with passengers on the way to Cancun.

Presented with these two alternatives, Keith had started to undress.

All the passengers, nine with Keith included, are dressed in black Kevlar now. Keith feels the vertigo of déjà vu as he reaches behind his back to tug on the parachute capsule strapped there.

On one of the seats, arranged like a rose on a handkerchief, Keith's favourite artificial foot rests on the sweaty t-shirt he has just taken off. One of the athletic-looking guys had handed Keith a crude pink plastic replacement that looked Victorian, all rusty springs and leather straps.

"Sorry, best we could do at short notice. We'll get you a better one back at base," the guy had explained earnestly.

***

Air traffic control had received a Mayday distress call from AN767 to Houston, while the plane was still over Mexican airspace. The pilot had informed ground control they had suffered a collision and explosion and had shut down number two port engine. They were descending to compensate for a loss of cabin pressure.

The flight was re-routed to San Antonio, where the emergency response teams were put on standby.

Forty minutes later, an explosion in the other port engine forces the pilot to take emergency action, turning the plane around to head back to Cotulla, where there is an airfield that might suffice.

They will never make it. The pilot—running out of options as the plane struggles to maintain altitude, fires burning throughout its cabin, shedding debris like dandruff—will try to make an emergency landing on the highway. With full thrust on the starboard engines and flaps and rudder fully locked to compensate for the port drag, the plane will be virtually un-flyable. Unable to keep the disintegrating mass of burning metal under control, the tumbling vehicle will crash into an industrial estate, destroying several buildings and incinerating the surroundings in a spectacular fireball. There will be no survivors.

Keith is second to last. All the nasty things that are likely to happen in the next few minutes present themselves for his conscious inspection. He considers them all, visualising them incarnate as violent fates circling the plane, waiting to take his frail body and rip it into fleshy strips.

'Fuck 'em,' he thinks to himself, steeling for action. How bad can it be? He has done worse, seen worse, been worse. He smiles. It must be adrenalin or endorphins, but he actually feels pretty cool.

They are in the luggage hold, surrounded by containers stuffed with suitcases and bags. The hatch is open, and the door long gone, ripped off by the screeching hurricane outside. Half a dozen black, boxy objects with fins, are pushed out first. Then, one after another, the crew departs through the sucking hole. Dee gives him the thumbs-up before it's her turn to exit. When Keith is up, he crouches in the opening, feeling the wind tugging at his arms and

191

head. Car headlights move along the freeway, and grids of streets are visible, picked out with orange or white street lighting. His military goggles—Spex, but harder core—show him airspeed, pick out his colleagues, and show a helpful green cross where he is expected to land.

Hands on his shoulders and he is out, tumbling through the night. In the first split second of chaotic confusion, the plane's tail passes way too close for comfort, scything through the black only metres away. He could clearly see the rivets and splattered insects frozen in the strobe light as it passed. The buffeting sends him cartwheeling and spinning, but instincts and unconscious muscle memory take over and he finds himself gliding. With a few adjustments, he is heading for his target. There is very little sound; active noise-cancelling buds take care of most of it and only a deep roar remains. He has difficulty finding the plane he recently departed. It is already over a kilometre away, but it will be back in twenty minutes to obliterate all traces of whatever it is they are here to do.

Keith watches the lead crew. The articulated, oversized, carbon-fibre *feathers* of their wings flare out, then a few dozen metres above the dessert their rocket boots fire. With augmented sight, he is able to follow their swoop and jogging landing.

Two nondescript office buildings are surrounded by a three-metre fence. There is a single guard post. The first two landers touch down around the corner of the building. They dash silently to the hut, where the guard is presumed to be watching late-night TV. The next four repeat the procedure, but instead of heading to the guard's hut, they go straight in through a side door and disappear into the building.

Keith has been paying too much attention to the action and is shocked when a shape looms out of the darkness next to him. He has been ignoring his target marker and needs to pull some mild aerobatics to point himself back in the right direction. He is heading for a cleared space a few hundred metres away from the fence, coming in at over a hundred miles per hour. The distance vanishes in an instant; just at the point where there is no doubt the chute has failed and he will be splattered on impact, he feels a huge surge of deceleration. Only fifty metres above the rapidly approaching ground, the high-tech active canopy deploys. The onboard computer dynamically changes the membrane's profile; it subjects him to an initial 5Gs, but this rapidly reduces—by the time he lands, the floor arrives with barely a nudge.

His chute whirs back into its lozenge. Drawing on years of training, he flicks into action, crossing the twenty or so metres to where the others are unpacking the boxy missiles that have landed safely. The finned boxes contain rucksacks and five folding electric dirt bikes. Keith gets straight to work assembling the bikes. His Spex display a large countdown in the top left-hand corner of his vision; it is showing a little over fourteen minutes by the time he joins the others.

The synthetic pilot, following the script, will have realised there is no chance of reaching San Antonio and will turn around, back to Cotulla, for its final fateful leg. Keith knows the next bit of the plan.

At eleven minutes, two of the crew return, dragging a

stumbling guard. One of the guys—Brian, Keith thinks he is called—pulls on a pair of jeans over his spandex suit trousers and pulls on a biker jacket. The guard is given a puffy red jacket and pink helmet. He is either a complete cretin or drugged, because he seems perfectly content to go while having his hands cuffed around Brian's waist. Both straddle the first of the newly assembled bikes. Brian gives a casual salute and they set off to the south.

At six minutes, the remaining four sprint back from the office building carrying several large, heavy black bags. The fence has already been carefully cut—links heated and stretched apart in a way consistent with participation in a tragic air disaster—allowing them to make straight for the rendezvous. Two more bikes head off after the first. Now, there are less than three minutes.

"Go now?" Keith hears a high-pitched synthesised voice squeak through his buds.

"Yeah, come here, you two," someone says affectionately. Two large black rats, apparently belonging to the inventory liberated from the office, are transferred into one of the rucksacks. The remaining crew get on bikes. Somehow, Keith gets to ride behind Dee, who is one of the final four.

"Did good? Get treat?" The squeaky voice coming in through Keith's Spex is politely synthetic—which, according to convention, indicates it belongs either to a machine or to an animal that doesn't mind sounding like a machine. Keith guesses it belongs to one of the rats.

"Very good, Freckles. You get a big treat!"

"Give treat."

"You need to wait; treat is not here. We will get the treat, okay?"

"Get treat now."

Keith looks around for some explanation, but the rats are clearly part of the team, and the others are too focused to chat. They set off at a sensible speed through the scrub, acutely aware of the mounting roar from the approaching airliner. Nothing showy, nothing risky, they still have a minute, and they only need to cover five hundred metres.

Zaki was at a critical point in his haggling, a heated vocal exchange, which had drawn in spectators from the neighbouring workshops. His opponent was a wiry, bearded man in filthy overalls.

"A thousand MeshCoins, Kemal! Come on, you've had them for months, what are you going to do with them anyway?"

"Zaki Kardesim, this is valuable resources. I sell in Constantinople for ten times what you say."

"One thousand five hundred then!"

"Why you want? Kaput, no more walk you say me."

They were in Kemal's workshop, a steel-framed polyhedron, walled with corrugated iron on the outskirts of the town's *Sani*. Dusty piles of wire and broken electronics were heaped around the walls. A small, formerly white caravan in one corner served as an office and, more often than not, also performed duty as Kemal's bedroom. A disassembled 4x4 was laid out carefully, like an exploded technical drawing. It shared the swept area in the middle of the workshop with a tangled, lifeless heap of limbs and bodies.

"Parts mostly. Good bits in them," Zaki attempted half-heartedly.

"Ha! No way, Zaki little brother," the man laughed, looking genuinely amused. "You are trying to scam your old friend Kemal!"

"Come on, Kemal. How about if Zaki manages to fix one up? How about if he gives it to you?"

Kemal raised an eyebrow. Zaki turned to glare at Siegfried, who was standing by the garage doors, where he had been told to wait and not interfere.

"They are broken. I told you. There is nothing I can do!" Zaki tried to rally, but he knew the damage was done. To be fair to Segi, Kemal was no fool and knew Zaki wouldn't be offering this much for spares.

Kemal sensed he had won and moved in for the kill. "Okay, it's a deal. Three thousand MeshCoin, and you give me one fixed suit!"

Zaki, grumbling, shook the grimy outstretched hand to seal the deal. They were invited for another tea, but decided to head off instead. Kemal, now humming a cheerful little ditty, would deliver the suits to their farm later in the day.

Segi and Zaki walked back up the narrow, sloping alley in silence, Zaki refusing to let his brother off the hook for screwing things up. However, despite acting annoyed, he was secretly thrilled to have managed to buy the heap of scrap he hoped to turn into half a dozen functional, bipedal automatons.

More than anything else, he had been afraid Kemal wouldn't take him seriously. Haggling in Osmanian at the bazaar felt like something of a rite of passage. He had originally thought about asking Granny to come and lurk menacingly in the background to add a dose of authenticity, but had decided it was time for him to man up.

Another reason for acting pissed off with Segi was to cover up his fear of explaining to his kinmates that he had blown a huge chunk of liquid assets on what, all grand schemes aside, was still a mound of scrap.

This was partly why he hadn't roped his great aunt or mother into the enterprise. When they tried to explain the Clan to their mother, they always described it as a sort of club for kids interested in computers or messing around with hardware. This was vaguely true but, depending on one's point of view, it could equally well be seen as an organised crime syndicate or paramilitary organisation.

After putting together and presenting a cool business case at Silicium's most recent virtual meet-up, Zaki had been authorised to use funds from the Clan's collective piggy bank for his project; but, in a slight departure from plan, he had just spent twice the agreed amount.

It was not quite stealing and would probably be okay—their clan had its fingers in many lucrative pies and, because it dealt mainly in Coin, it was always looking for ways to invest its capital in tangible assets. The two teenagers were established members, they had healthy reputation numbers from contributing to the BugNet codebase and from the thousands of MeshNodes they had distributed around the Anatolian countryside over the past few years.

They also had income from their ever-expanding bioreactor setup. Hydrogen gas, carbon-fibre ribbon and other products were grown within the trellises of transparent tubes that snaked their way around the smallholding. GliderKites delivered the production to faraway places, while dropping MeshNodes into black spots as they soared silently, kilometres up, above the skirmishes and confusion of the Caliphate's perpetually changing borders. All this revenue made the brothers a good investment—but there was always a chance that somebody in the leadership would be more interested in the principle than the bottom line, and drop high-altitude ballistic penetrators through them as an example to others.

On Saturdays, the marketplace would be packed with vegetable stalls and cheese sellers. Today, it was mostly empty, and the big cobbled square was being used by a group of kids playing football. The brothers drank tea and ate baklava, seated at an old iron table at the edge of the marketplace.

They met Kemal again at 3 pm and drove in his old, battered truck to the Çiftlik house. Together, they awkwardly unloaded the suits from the back of the lorry, where they were hidden under a rubberised tarpaulin. As quickly as possible, considering the weight and the unpredictable way the limbs of the suits wildly swung, the boys lugged them across the yard to safe cover in the old barn. Zaki had checked the overhead times for satellites, but still wanted them out of sight as quickly as possible.

***

From the drone's elevated vantage point, the approaching vehicles were almost obscured by billowing clouds of dust spewed up by their wheels. A modern auto leading, an ancient *dolmush* bouncing along behind. Zaki had pinged Siegfried and, together, they had frenetically hidden, or at least pulled tarpaulin over, anything considered contraband by either the ZKF or the Caliphate. Their mother had flatly refused to get into the cellar as a precaution, and they hadn't even bothered asking Granny—even the suggestion would have been guaranteed a playful and agonising pinch of the cheek and an equally painful soul-baring glare. So, when the soldiers rolled up to the gate, they were greeted by two frosty, black-clad widows.

An olive-uniformed, middle-aged officer climbed out of the sleek auto. On the drive from the town, he had tried to recall the face of the old woman. He had explored the crumbling arches and overgrown orange groves as a boy. The woman had seemed terrifyingly old then, throwing her decomposing lemons at the trespassing kids. Now, she must be ancient.

A couple of scruffy soldiers jumped out of the knackered bus and immediately lit cigarettes. Kemal stayed sitting in the back, his hands cuffed. He had a nasty bruise covering the right side of his face and a smear of red across his lips and nose.

Zaki and Segi had shuttered the big barn and were monitoring things from their workshop, scanning the feeds from assets around the estate. They knew they existed precariously, neutral in the skirmishes that surrounded them. They were not helpless, but it was always better not to have to show your hand. Buying the junked combat armour had been a risk, and now it seemed the ZKF had somehow learnt of the transaction and wanted in on the battlesuit action.

Aal stood behind her gate, arms folded on top, frowning

and glaring at the approaching soldiers. When he spoke, the officer was polite and deferential, as was correct when speaking to the lady of the house, but Aal wasn't having any of whatever he was selling. Zaki couldn't hear, but it wasn't much of a leap to assume the conversation had something to do with his recent purchase. Aal had never seen the things, and Zaki was sure she wouldn't have a clue what the man was talking about or why she should care. She was, however, sure they would not come onto her property.

Now, she was squinting and muttering, while pointing back and forth between the soldiers and the blue glass eye hanging off the gate. Zaki couldn't help but smile. He almost clapped his hands. The old woman was going to curse them.

Ayşe, standing behind, had taken a bunch of herbs out of a pocket in her apron and passed them forward. These were lit, and a thick yellow smoke, following a fortuitous wind, began to drift towards the vehicles. The continued bombardment of powerful and ancient curses seemed to be having an effect. The officer took a couple of steps back, while the soldiers flapped with their hands and moved clumsily away from the drifting smoke, which seemed to be capriciously following them.

Now was the perfect opportunity to use the 'dread ray', a device which caused terror, or, on lower settings, a smouldering dread. It was non-lethal and, if used correctly, enemies would not even know they had been attacked. Essentially, it was a powerful phased array transmitter and thousand-watt PA that could send a strong, pulsing electromagnetic field and accompanying wall of infrasound. The carefully modulated magnetic fields would mess with the head, while the infrasound could literally empty the bowels. It had been surprisingly easy to build from plans floating around the Mesh. When used on low power, it produced a creeping dread and sense of impending doom. Unless the victim was expecting the attack, or was familiar with the weapon, the resultant qualia were usually attributed to external, often supernatural, sources.

The big device looked like a garden fork with too many prongs, crossed with a 1950s ray gun. The brothers moved the accompanying speakers into position and started it on low power, aiming it through the obscuring wooden walls of the barn towards the soldiers' vehicles. The two ladies knew what was coming, but still involuntarily tightened and glanced around for reassurance when the switch was flipped and the hairs on the backs of their necks stood on end.

The officer, already uncomfortable with orders telling him to come up here and bother the well-respected old matron, began to experience a conviction that he was committing some horrible crime against Allāh. Divine disapproval was manifesting as a physical weight on his shoulders and a churning in his stomach. He felt a skeletal hand inside his shirt, clenching his heart. The smells of the fumes and the evil cursing were enough; he began to edge away from the gate. The sky was ochre with smoke. Soldiers inside the bus began a nervous chittering.

When he heard the percussive metallic sounds of weapons being fiddled with, the officer decided to pull back. He could feel the sense of panic spreading. The skittish men would do something stupid if he didn't get them away.

They sped back to town, leaving ghosts and the two terrifying women to raise their boys alone.

The boys laughed, despite the tongue lashing they would shortly be receiving for bringing soldiers to the house in the first place.

Five of the battlesuits looked in good shape; another two were badly damaged, with missing limbs and nasty, fatal-looking wounds in their armour. Another three were scrap. They had all come from the tiltrotor that had crashed back in the Spring. Kemal had headed over to loot the wreckage, expecting nothing more than scrap metal, and perhaps some live ammunition. He had hit the jackpot, but hadn't known what to do with the battlesuits. He had kept quiet for months, until Zaki, who had heard a rumour, turned up with his offer to take the scrap off his hands.

Zaki insisted they had been set up; but, despite agreeing that word had somehow spread back to the local ZKF leadership, Kemal swore he had kept the deal a secret. Eventually, they agreed that he could keep the payment, and they would even forgive him and not offer him up to the Clan for retribution—if he offered the three write-offs, stripped of crucial spare parts, to the technically illiterate ZKF militia and convinced them there was nothing of value up at the Çiftlik house to justify another visit.

A few nights later, as Zaki was working on the suits, he realised that one of the anthropoid shells would have once belonged to Keith. Not for the first time, he wondered what the reluctant soldier hero was up to now...

'Probably drunk on a beach somewhere!' he laughed to himself, grinning in the dim light of the barn while twisting off a damaged foot.

The screaming, flaming wreck arrives like an avenging angel roaring out of the sky to bring retribution on the Earth. It strikes the ground twenty metres or so from the edge of the fence and transforms into a cone of destruction. Sequentially, fence, guard house, and office building are simply erased. A split second after impact, there is a brain-pulverising concussion as a mist of vaporised kerosene, released on impact, combusts, sending up a not so mini mushroom cloud. Keith is looking back, watching the spectacle. They are over a kilometre away, but the shockwave is still considerable. The timer disappears from his Spex and is replaced by an arrow and a new number: forty kilometres.

"Okay, now that we seem to have a few minutes, any chance you can tell me what the FUCK is going on?"

Dee answers by banging her helmet against Keith's visor. Obviously, she doesn't feel like elaborating at the moment.

The electric off-road bikes are relatively silent as they bump through the desert, big soft tyres rolling easily over scrub and stones.

"Satellite will be over in six minutes," a voice says over the group channel. "There is a drone en route; at current speed, it will be over us in twenty-two. What's your status, Brian?"

"In three or four minutes I join the thirty-five. I'll take it from here. Good luck, guys."

"Copy that. Everybody else pull in together. Mindy, be

ready with the camo."

"Roger," a female voice confirms.

Up ahead, one of the bikes has stopped, again without drama; no skidding, no dust. Two people, one of them presumably Mindy, quickly shakes open a huge blanket with ragged fractal edges. It's silvered on the underside, with mottled camo on the top. The other three remaining bikes gently pull up and nudge underneath. They wait. Radios and bike motors are turned off. Nobody speaks—which doesn't really make sense to Keith, but he doesn't dare bring it up in case there *is* some way satellites in space can listen to voices.

"That's it. We're good. Still twelve minutes until the drone gets here."

The bikes head off again, perhaps another two kilometres of bumping through the scrub, and then they surge up a small ramp and turn onto a rough tarmac road that merges on either side with the dusty orange. There is very little traffic on the road. The few cars they pass have pulled over to watch the towering fireball that is fading, but still looms, over them. They are close enough to see that the air is full of burning confetti, and they can hear explosions when pockets of kerosene or hydraulic fluid go up in flames.

Two bikes stop near a cluster of vehicles, where a guy in a baseball cap and stained vest is standing on the roof of an ancient wrecked mini-bus parked, or possibly abandoned, at the side of the road. He is excitedly shouting a blow by blow description of what he can see to his friends. As Keith and Dee pass, Keith sees Mindy join the shouted conversation with the guy on the roof.

The drone will be overhead now. Keith and Dee are riding about half a kilometre behind Terrance and Chuck on the lead bike. Brian has taken the delirious guard south, possibly towards Mexico. Keith hopes they are not going to kill him and lose the body in some overgrown creek. Mindy and three other jumpers have parked their bikes and are blending in with the rubbernecking rednecks. Even from the drone's enhanced point of view, there should be nothing unusual or suspicious to flag. Time will tell if the multiple layers of subterfuge will resist careful analysis, but, at the very least, it should buy them enough time to get out of the area.

"Package is secure, heading to rendezvous."

"Copy that," Dee says, glancing up at the lead bike. To Keith she says, "We should be okay now. We will be at the next rendezvous in less than an hour. If anything goes down, we are support for Terence and Chuck. They have the package. They need to get out. We don't, okay?"

"Okay, got you," says Keith. "Expendable is my middle name."

"There is a pistol in the side pocket of your pack," says Dee. "Don't feel you need to kill yourself if we get captured, though. You don't know anything, anyway."

"Wow! I'd forgotten how much fun you are."

Dee bangs her helmet against his visor again, but this time it is almost affectionate.

Their bike shudders along the rough tarmac. Dangerously over-capacity and irritated by the constant vibration, Keith's bladder is at DEFCON 1: COCKED PISTOL; nuclear war is imminent. His erection, not willing to sit out the crisis entirely, is operating at DEFCON 3: ROUND HOUSE; increase in force readiness above that required by normal circumstances.

It is the catsuit that Keith can't get out of his mind. The jeans and jacket Dee pulled on top before they set off are a mere superficial irrelevance, beneath which, he knows, mounds, valleys and flat expanses of tantalising black Lycra lie, like the terrain of an undiscovered planet. A tiny part of Keith's mind—the part which is not currently occupied dealing with all the neurological sirens, blaring klaxons, strobing lights, emergency flares, alarm bells, screaming wardens, and intermittent sharp slaps to the face being broadcast in a constant barrage by his distraught organs—is curious to see whether BLADDER prevails and manages to squeeze its liquid payload past PENIS's vigilant clenched checkpoints, or whether PENIS will be able to maintain full launch readiness until a fountain of piss bursts out of Keith's ears with the force of a ruptured fire hose.

As the 'distance to destination' readout counts down to zero, they cruise unmolested along mostly empty roads. The land on either side is virtually deserted, with only a few clusters of buildings or solar farms breaking the monotony. A couple of times, emergency vehicles pass with sirens and lights blazing. Their physical presence is preceded by warnings and instructions broadcast into the digital.

Dee pulls off the road at a bleached wooden sign announcing showers and 'low, low rates'. They follow more guidance overlays to a big old RV, where they pull up beside Terence and Chuck, who are dusting off. Helmets are lifted and grins exchanged.

Keith dismounts carefully and—ignoring the querying glances from Dee and the others—walks stiffly out of view around the side of the RV. There he stands, eyes closed, beads of sweat pricking his forehead, vibrating with effort, while he fumbles with his zippers and eventually manages to retrieve his suffering organ and aim it away from his body.

He clearly hears a heavenly choir exalting hallelujah as he allows himself to relax; then, he is almost knocked off his feet by recoil as a golden beam of energy blasts from his groin.

When it is over, Keith returns to his body, seals up his suit and re-joins the others. He gets the impression that they stopped their conversation some time ago and have just been standing, slack-jawed, as shadows lengthen, listening to Keith pressure washing the resonant metallic skin of the RV.

"What?" Keith says, stepping over a new stream which looks like it is spiritedly embarking on a journey to reach the sea.

More immediate action follows. First, hosing the bikes down, presumably washing off any stubborn traces of air disaster, then the bikes are hung up and hooked to the back of the RV.

Inside, they strip off everything that screams 'tactical' and stuff it into a big, dark green, wheelie suitcase. The two rats are pulled out, and Terence places them lovingly on the floor. He spends a minute kneeling down, tickling them behind the ears, and feeding them chunks of dried mango. Eventually, the rats hop out the door and down the steps.

"Don't be long!" Terence calls after them.

During the unpacking, a rough, oval, metal object, with thick wires sticking out of one end, is carefully transferred from a padded, military-looking grey plastic case into a shoulder bag that might conceivably be used for carrying archaic pieces of photographic equipment.

"That's it then, is it? The package?" Keith asks.

Ignoring him, Dee says, "Let's get a few hours of sleep. We'll set off in the morning at eight-thirty. Chuck, fill Keith in on the plan."

"Right, cover story," says Chuck. "We are two couples on holiday. You're both in there." Chuck points to a door behind them. "Me and Terry are here on the pull-out. We bought this beauty in Los Angeles," he says, slapping the wall of the RV, "and we're heading for New Orleans. Details are here..." He pings Keith a tarball that registers, jiggling on the *shelf* briefly, before fading into Keith's peripheral vision.

Keith raises both eyebrows and turns his head to check with Dee, but she has already turned away and is opening the door to what Keith gathers is their shared bedroom. Clearly, that's all.

Terence and Chuck look at him briefly, then turn to each other, embrace and start kissing passionately. Keith gets the feeling they are not having to act too hard at being a couple. He decides to give them some space and follows Dee. The room is very cramped, basically a bed and a small area of floor inside the door that has recently become strewn with what appears to be *all* of Dee's clothes—although he can't confirm this hypothesis, as only her head is visible protruding out from under the duvet.

"They are taking their roles seriously!" Keith says, looking around the room and trying to work through the logistics of the situation.

"Infrared," Dee replies, pointing up through the ceiling. "Satellites. But they're always like that after action. Chuck is like the most professional soldier you will ever meet, then when he's off duty, he's a complete bimbo."

"Okay, right. So that's them sorted, and you have a bed..." Keith says, making a show of looking around the tiny room. He locks eyes and then continues, "and where should I...?"

Face utterly impassive, maintaining eye contact the whole time, Dee shifts over a smidgen.

***

The next day, Chuck is wearing shorts and a flowery shirt and looks like he just washed up after a glorious wipe-out. He is driving, while Terence, Dee, and Keith sit around in the lounge area behind him. They are relaxed and look like they have not a care in the world, but Keith witnesses Chuck's transformation into clipped speech and military demeanour when an opportunity arises to dispose of the incriminating suitcase. They are crossing a low pontoon bridge above a wide finger of reservoir. They slow down, almost to a halt, then toss the case out through the RV's sliding door. It disappears below the green water in a single viscous swallow. Chuck, back to surfer dude, stamps the accelerator, and they trundle away.

Keith had woken in the morning to find that his legs and neck had been bitten to pieces by mosquitoes. Terence has some Aloe vera. Dee just finds it hilarious, remarking helpfully that she had been completely ignored by the insects, while they feasted on Keith.

Terence, who seems to be the team's medic and vet, reels off some of CuliCo Corp's marketing material. Apparently, their NoBiteU™ mosquito is incapable of biting 90% of people. After a little mental arithmetic, Keith points out that, in practice, this leaves one in ten people shouldering the entire parasitic load. This leads into a discussion on the whole concept of *Recognising Economic Value of Beneficial Species*. They sip their truck stop coffees and openly and enthusiastically share their opinions of CuliCo Corp and the efficacy of REVOBS:

"It's bullshit."

"That's a bit simplistic, Keith," Terence offers.

"No, he's right Terry. The people pay like five per cent of their taxes to that crap. It's subsidies for bullshit mosquitoes, wasps, and jellyfish!" Chuck calls from up front.

"Guys," says Dee. "Right now, man is causing one of the planet's greatest mass extinctions. We have to protect whatever is left, whatever the personal cost to some of us. Keith, you should feel privileged to have the opportunity to do your bit for bio-diversity."

Keith glares at her.

"Come on, Keith. It's an itchy neck, man up!" Chuck suggests. "And anyway, you'll get a pay-out for the blood."

It was true. CuliCo Corp would happily transfer 0.000001 of a MeshCoin into his wallet as compensation if he just took the twenty minutes necessary to complete the claim.

"Okay, I've had worse. It's not the neck, although if I could read braille, I think I might find the entire mosquito bible written there," Keith says, putting on a brave face. "It's just another big bag of bollocks, right? That's what gets me. Another mess wrapped in layers of bullshit double talk. I'm sick of it. But, sorry. Hey, what about you guys? What do you do on Atlantis? I can't imagine Niato lets himself get bitten. I can't see him slathering on the DEET to keep the buggers away, either, though. I bet he's got some Gaian Earth Mother solution, right? Teach them all Buddhism, maybe?"

"Terry, you told me about this one. We don't have mosquitoes, do we?" Chuck says.

"Nope, no mosquitoes. We incentivise the natural ecosystems to remove them."

The rats are back, and Terence produces jerky from his pocket, giving one large piece to each of them.

"What the hell does that mean?" Keith asks.

"Okay, so where to start?" replied Terence. "Do you know what the Mesh is? Yes, sure, of course you do. Sorry. So, on Atlantis we have another network alongside it which ties all the local animals into a sort of economy where they can contribute, add value and, in return, earn rewards."

"Err, one time a grasshopper saved my life," Keith says, dragging up the only fragment which seems to relate.

"Really? Cool."

"Yeah, showed up and led me to two little hacker kids. It saved my life after I got my foot shot off, then had a plane crash on top of me."

"It was hardly on top of you," Dee says.

"Oh, I see. No, not that one. This was another completely different plane a little while ago. I can see how that might have been confusing. No, this one was RIGHT on top of me. Very nasty. I nearly died. So yes, there we go. Where were we? So, I ended up in a psychiatric hospital, was not in a good way for a while. Then these hacker guys sprung me, so that I could rescue their friend from pirates."

"Whoa! Man, that's some crazy shit right there!" Chuck says, swivelling backwards again, clearly impressed enough that he forgets about the road for a worrying amount of time.

"Niato didn't tell me all that," Dee says, looking at Keith curiously.

"It's all been a bit stressful recently, to tell the truth," says

Keith. "I was really looking forward to this trip to Cancun to unwind..."

"Ha, hilarious! And then we turn up and drag you out of an exploding plane to steal a nuclear bomb!"

"Chuck, you twat!" says Terence, clapping his palm to his face.

"Oh, fuck, sorry," says Chuck. "I forgot—need to know, right?"

"A what?!"

"It's not a bomb!" Dee says, glaring at Chuck.

"It's not?" says Chuck, again facing the wrong way. He is clearly not used to travelling in vehicles not capable of driving themselves.

"Chuck, can you please focus on driving? And let's try to get back to a bit of operational discipline, okay?"

"Yes, Ma'am, copy that," he says, turning his chair back to a forward-facing aspect and assuming his military persona.

Dee and Terence exchange a look.

"Keith," Dee then says, "for your piece of mind, it's not a bomb, and it's not radioactive—at least, not very. And honestly, it's better that you don't know anything else. Okay?"

"Fine. So what about the mosquitoes, then? Or is that

classified above my level too?"

Terence looks at Dee again, then says, "Actually, it probably is, but it sounds like you already have some first-hand experience. I'm guessing these friends of yours were Kinfolk?"

"Silicium."

"So, being rescued by a Kin grasshopper probably puts you inside the fence here. What do you say, Dee?"

"We can always just kill him if he can't keep his mouth shut," Dee offers.

"Thanks for that," Keith says, looking back to Terence in the hope of more constructive input.

"The BugNet is basically the Internet of Animals," Terence explains. "Special little MeshNodes scattered around, ready to be eaten by rats, cats, crows, whatever… you get the picture. They interface with the animal's body by growing into their brains and optic nerves. It gives the animal something like Spex, and if you get them young enough, they can learn a language of symbols."

"Electronic brain parasites? That doesn't sound very Earth Mother to me!"

"I know. I always found that bit a little icky. But once integrated, we can interact with them, communicate, and they can communicate with each other."

"You are not going to tell me you make cyborg mosquitoes and then ask them not to bite people?"

"No, insects are too basic to communicate with symbols."

"And my grasshopper?"

"Probably just remote controlled."

"Okay. So, I still can't quite see how this works."

"It's pretty basic economics, really," continues Terence. "We pay the BugNet to kill mosquitoes."

"Come again?"

"Mosquitoes are tagged in the BugNet to be removed and given a financial reward value. I imagine they are high-lighted, somehow, to the chipped critter…"

"The lucky furry fucker who ate the brain chip, right?" Chuck asks.

"Yeah, that's it," replies Terence. "So, let's say a mosquito flies past, in the animal's vision it gets tagged, like Spex overlays. The animal learns it will get a reward if it eats the mosquito. So, it does, and receives some credits it can spend at vending machines across the islands."

"Are you telling me, mice are queuing up to buy cheese at a vending machine with their mosquito bounty?" asks Keith.

"Well, in the case of mosquitoes, the vigilantes are mostly bats, and they tend to buy crickets with their Coin. But essentially, yes."

The RV cruises on. They plunge through utterly deserted towns. Cab-less delivery trucks, oblongs on tiny wheels, make up 90% of the road traffic, trundling between warehouses and scruffy little homes with overgrown gardens. The delivery bots are non-judgemental towards the blinking, overweight, digital-displacees, who brave brief forays into the environment to pick up their care packages.

In the South, even before global warming turned up the thermostat, reliance on air conditioning had always kept most of the productive activity confined to the interiors of buildings. For journeys between enclaves of protected environment, cars provided mobile bubbles of clement climate. Now that digital travel—game spaces and shared geometries—had made most journeys unnecessary, RL was becoming depopulated.

Terence had scooted up front with Chuck, leaving Keith and Dee to chat in the lounge section. She seems genuinely interested, so he catches her up on the last few years of his life. She has seen her fair share of violence as Niato's go-to girl for special projects, but she still looks shocked as Keith recounts details from his stint policing Europe's many ongoing listless genocides.

From Dee, Keith gathers that Niato has a lot of irons in the fire and that the to-do list for a new monarch out to save the world is long and eclectic.

The scenery remains flat, and Keith is surprised when they suddenly pull up next to a bleached wooden jetty, sticking out into a narrow creek. Chuck and Terence swivel their chairs backwards, and Dee gets up and starts boiling water in the little kettle.

Terence opens the door, and the rats appear from wherever they have been slinking and bound out. The door is left open, despite what Keith estimates is a high probability of mosquito visitation.

"Can't we shut the door?"

"Nope, got to listen. Our contact might be early," Dee replies.

"What's next then?" Keith asks.

"Okay, so Chuck and I will continue on to New Orleans," Terence explains. "You and Dee will hop out here. It's too much trouble getting people in and out of CONUS since they went all paranoid, so we don't get to go home, sob sob. We will just have to lurk around here somewhere, until we are needed again. Few weeks in New Orleans sound good to you, Chucky?"

"I think I could survive it," he smiles.

Dee brings over four cups of green tea, a bunch of bananas and a family-sized bag of crisps. There is a definite tension. They don't want to worry him, but Keith gets the impression this is a crucial part of the plan. A rat hops back up the stairs and 'says' something to Terence.

"Looks like they are here!" Terence says with obvious relief.

The others jump out of their chairs and head out. Keith follows. Chuck goes back the way they have just driven, tucking a functional black pistol into the back of his trousers as he goes. Dee and Terence walk towards the water. Keith looks around for their contact; he can't hear a motor yet.

One of the rats is swimming towards them, its furry body undulating and its tiny paws scratching at the water. Keith becomes aware that there is something else in the water. A bulge announces the arrival of a large, sleek muzzle. Keith wants to call out and warn the little animal, but before he can say anything, it surfaces under the rat and raises it smoothly out of the water, carrying it shoreward.

There are three more. They each have a pair of something like long, low, waterproof rucksacks symmetrically strapped to their flanks.

Keith shouldn't really have been surprised at the nature of the extraction team. The plan becomes clear as they unpack two streamlined dry-suits and scuba cylinders. The contoured helmets, with what can only be described as nostrils on the top, look more like alien spacesuits than diving gear.

"When we are at the surface, the helmet will suck in and compress fresh air," Dee explains. "If you don't move too much, we should have a good hour's supply, just in case we need to sink and lurk for a while."

The mysterious egg is stowed in one of the emptied dolphin-packs.

The dolphins will be their steeds and scouts, pulling them out of Baffin Bay into the Gulf of Mexico. Silent, invisible, and deniable. Eighty nautical miles will be exhausting for the humans and presumably not much fun for the human-towing dolphins. If compromised, the terrestrial mammals will be left to flounder, while the cetaceans make a dash for open ocean with the precious nuclear-not-a-bomb.

If all goes to plan, the humans will slip on board a friendly vessel offshore and start the journey to Bäna and the Kingdom. The low-value assets, Dee and Keith, will take the shortcut through the Panama Canal. The pod of special-ops dolphins will take the long way around, until they reach safer waters.

After a surprisingly emotional farewell, Keith and Dee wade into the bay. The dolphins are chittering excitedly, craning their big grinning heads from side to side out of the water. A sort of lie-down saddle replaces one of the dolphin-packs, and a harness clips them on for when exhausted arms give way.

CHAPTER 14 – ACTIVITY THEORY

Picture an intercontinental freeway network, decaying within the borders of a failed state. A post-apocalyptic web of cracked tarmac and fallen overpasses. Armed convoys thunder through the scenery, while gangs of thugs on spiky choppers daub themselves in war paint and speed alongside or lurk in cracks and shadows, ready for cryptographic ambush. This is the internet. For corporations who can afford the table fee in kickbacks and quantum encryption modules, it is the only game in town. Its routers, switches, cables, fibres, and satellite networks still carry a trillion times the capacity of the Mesh. It remains the only viable option for transporting bulk data at any sensible speed and cost.

The crumbling world wide web built on top has itself become a metaphorical anarchy of towering wrecks and drifting tear gas. Surfing the web with a standard Companion or old school laptop is the equivalent of pulling on a pink Lycra bodysuit and going for a late evening jog through the ghetto.

Most users only visit the internet's manicured corporate enclaves, spending their time in the saccharine theme parks, which cower behind firewalls and government key escrow inspection checkpoints.

Glitches and leaks are business as usual. Porn-bot flash-mobs a constant annoyance. Malicious agents rattle the bars and swarm in through exploits of their own—or, more often, opportunistically follow in the wake of raids by entities higher up the food chain.

In comparison, the Mesh is a backwater of rural lanes and cycle paths. Community maintained and fully distributed.

Software agents negotiate passage and deal with the tedious onion layers of signatures and keys. The full power of asymmetric maths—open-sourced and generally considered to be free of government backdoors—protects data in-flight, while heterogeneous infrastructure and distributed routing make it a costly, low-value target for attack. It is slow and unreliable. Limited bandwidth makes it vulnerable to saturation. During major internet storms or corporate skirmishes, the fat pipe traffic from the Super-Highway forces its way down to the capillaries of the Mesh—prices soar and transmission speeds slow to a crawl.

The Mesh is a Fully Autonomous Corporation, or FAC. It is governed by the emergent consensus of impartial algorithms that calculate fees, and flocks of unsupervised agents, which rate journey experience. Payment for passage can only be bought with its own inflationary MeshCoins, which are mined at each physical edge and routing node. The transient ephemeral nature of the Mesh has pieces dropping offline continuously. The Coin generation algorithms focus on performance, incentivising the crowd to fill in blank spots and constantly build out capacity.

MeshCoin; always in demand, inflation keeps it liquid, distributed infrastructure ensures its independence, its value is backed by the worth of the entire Mesh. It is, quite simply, the world's favourite currency and, lately, it has begun piling up in Stella's virtual piggy bank in life-changing quantities…

She looked up from her toenails as her Companion vibrated and signalled that another full Coin had been deposited. Twice over the last few months, she had changed the sensitivity of the alert when the constant beeping had become too annoying. Her toenails were now 80% matte white.

The little toes were still *au naturel*, and she was wondering if her fans would approve if she painted them black. She considered putting it to a vote, but couldn't be bothered. Anyway, she had been told not to pander to them too much, or they would become intolerable and lose interest. 'Keep them wanting more', the studio avatar had instructed her.

Her life was predominantly nocturnal. Her skin was pale. She had kept out of the sun since her ordeal in the dark. Her hair was gone; she maintained the internal firewall and refused to remember screaming for scissors and brutally cutting the dirty dreads away.

She looked at herself in the hotel mirror. The wig of chunky white rectangular fibres made her look like a low-polygon NPC. The boy sitting on the bed gave her a thumbs-up. Her new, high-end, white pearl Companion signalled again from the dresser; another Coin. A succession of brief sub-vocalised thoughts through her Spex, and she decreased the sensitivity of the alert again.

Perhaps the fembot look was too contrived. It was far from the practical-but-elegant style she preferred; but she was doing something right, the fans approved and Coins poured in. Taking the little brush between her fingers, with controlled parallel strokes, she completed her toes.

***

"Jeno, a little privacy, please."

The *oid* boy flicked his hair away from his eyes theatrically, then moodily got up and walked towards the suite's other room. As Stella took off her Spex, his shape blurred and flickered, then glitched out as the Spex lasers gave up trying to project him onto her retinas. She could barely see his tiny tele-presence bee, but she assumed its cameras were no longer looking her way. The command for privacy should anyway block all outgoing streams. She took off the hotel dressing gown and avoided the mirror as she slipped her arms and head into a new white Kimono-smock. It was expensive, made from ersatz spider silk. Her oversized Otaku Spex and chunky grey utility belt completed the outfit.

Jeno coughed, time to stream again. Privacy pauses may keep fans engaged, reminding them they are consuming a premium resource, but go dark for too long, and the attention-deficit teenagers will shift focus and may never come back. Jeno acted like her boyfriend, but he was more like her producer and cameraman. Fundamentally, though, he was a virtual personality. For the cameras, they were supposed to be an item. She had been coached to treat him like her boyfriend, but to make sure their relationship remained platonic. Secretly, the fans dreamt of meeting her and, one day, falling in love.

However, it was not just her they were after. Many saw her as the competition and hoped to woo Jeno. The cognitive dissonance and suspension of disbelief required was beyond Stella. He was an *oid*, a virtual avatar without a physical form. didn't even own his own software; his personality was assembled from timeshare slices of commodity algorithms, running in BHJ data centres. The only physical part of him was the tiny tele-presence camera bee that captured his simulated POV as he streamed the banal details of her life across the Mesh.

Shortly after she had shuffled off the coastguard launch wrapped in a silverised disaster blanket, Jeno had materialised and offered to keep all the drones and paparazzi away. Keith had been ready to take her home, her tickets already booked; but, mentally fractured and suffering from post-traumatic shock, Stella had declined his offer.

She had fought and screamed and thrashed against the pirates when they snatched her. Then, the shock of seeing Marcel getting shot had sent her away to another place. Violence and months below deck, surrounded by sobbing hopeless human flesh, had sealed her in her own mental room. Each day, the walls between herself and the hopeless reality beyond her mind had grown higher and thicker.

The ordeal was fading. It was months since she stepped off the coastguard boat and into the blazing light of celebrity. Yet, despite the time that had passed, she was still there locked in her cell. Going home to the Farm would force her to come out and confront it all, so she continued to block incoming calls, avoiding contact with her friends and all thoughts of home.

When she felt weak and self-indulgent, she pulled up the analytics. Hundreds of calls were still being screened every day by her TeenLife™ Sages. Most would be other Life Agencies or miscellaneous propositions at various grades of respectability. Chris was still calling every couple of weeks. He was the only one to whom she had sent any communication, a simple note saying she was okay, but needed time. Marcel had stopped calling after a week of being ignored.

Her friends in Zilistan still couldn't comprehend the rejection. She knew the brothers must feel betrayed and spurned after rescuing her, but they couldn't understand she wasn't the same person anymore.

Standing on the harbour, surrounded by smiling faces, target for lenses broadcasting her shame to millions, she had wanted to fold herself away and leave the world. So, instead of dragging her humiliation home with her, she had accepted Jeno's offer and consented—by degrees—to have her life turned into a reality show.

With jealous and judicious application of their legal department, TeenLife™ had stilled the clamour of demanding voices and put her inside a bubble in the eye of a media storm.

She grabbed her Companion and dropped it into one of the belt's plush pockets. Jeno waited for her to open the door, and they left the suite. The fans wanted action; they wanted glamour and an aspirational lifestyle.

The lift dropped and her ears popped before the doors slid silently open. The elevators discharged into recessed arches on the perimeter of a wide, shallow terraced bowl. Scarlet velvet ropes separated the tiers. At the bottom was the dance floor, already packed with milling, glittering bodies. A chaotic blend of AR projections and illuminated smart fabrics created a psychedelic kaleidoscope of barely human shapes. They skirted the upper rim, past the concierge desks, and headed to the lobby and the street exit beyond. A couple of heads followed them, but Stella was very much a niche celebrity. Her demographic was either too young to be allowed out after 8 pm, or too socially inadequate to be let in by the club's critical doormen.

Beyond an invisible cordon outside the hotel door, KL's night was just getting going. Faces with oversized eyes, scalps wriggling with sentient hair, bodies naked or adorned with shiny jewellery that wouldn't have looked out of place in a pharaoh's tomb. Some sported S&M thongs and studs. There was a smattering of Cosplay and the odd furry. Stella had to disable her Spex briefly to gauge what was real and what was AR. She was surprised at how much of the insanity was base reality, baryonic stuff, and light.

The city was simultaneously fleshy, dirty, glittering, and ethereal. A few shell-shocked huddles of men with beards and kurtas walked amongst the crazy. KL was famous for its lenience in applying the Caliph's edicts and, in a kind of anti-hajj, many of the faithful came expressly to ogle its decadence.

The pavements were crowded. However, as they walked between towering, neon-encrusted buildings, the masses avoided Jeno, steering around him as if he was a physical peer—unless they chose to be rude and barged through his incorporeal body, confident there would be no retaliation.

Stella maintained a hierarchy of worth. She placed all the laughing flesh and blood humans at the top, Sages and simulated personalities below, and herself at the bottom; broken and stretched out, a two-dimensional meniscus over a sucking sore.

She thought of her friends again, Segi and Zaki. Then she smiled at Jeno, incorporeal and emotionally superficial, the perfect *boyfriend*…

…other fragments of personality tried to rise from her subconscious to protest, but she shut them down before they could fully form.

Water filmed the faintly glowing rock. Rivulets, channelled by the topology of the cave's walls, meandered chaotically, while stray drops splashed the moss and liverworts which had taken root in the many cracks and fissures.

The tunnel gave the impression of age and of having once carried vast torrents of water. Now, the water was far below, but its roar still dominated the soundscape.

The adventurers fell into their standard formation and crept on into the grotto's sinuous deeps. Several times they came across clutches of small bones forming irregular pyramids on the smooth, undulating floor. Phalanges and metatarsals dumped by the dying vortices of recent floods. A thigh bone projected from where it had become wedged deep in a fissure, calcified growth cementing it in place and decorating its surface with ridges of fine scrimshaw.

The cabin boy, their scout, wandering carelessly ahead with no apparent consideration for stealth, disturbed a nest of lung-eels. A short skirmish ensued; cutlasses and breach-loading pistols eventually dispatching the annoying creatures. Unfortunately, not before needle-sharp spines had injected incapacitating poison through the pale skin of the cabin boy's bare ankle. Judging by the way he was stumbling and mumbling with delirium, he probably wouldn't make it much further.

Not-Captain NoBeard, the rag tag posse's leader, grumbled and pushed them on; there was nothing he could do. The cabin boy was toast. *NoBeard* had probably misjudged by not picking up an antidote, but they couldn't spend all their Coin on healing cabin boys. The party was too small. Chaloska, the ship's Voodoo priest, was still heartbroken and inconveniently absent. Without his magic, they were pitifully vulnerable.

Later, during a quiet interlude, they harvested rock crystal from a spectacular cavern then fought the mummy-boss-eel they found coiling about a chest in one of the many side chambers. They dispatched her without too much trouble, alternating between ranged attacks and close frenzied stabbing. Towards the end, when it should have all been over, the cabin boy took a flying spine in the neck and fell fitting into a pool of shallow water. His flailing limbs whipped blood and brine into a salty froth.

"Fuck! Not again!" *NoBeard* swore, watching the boy's movements become weak and sporadic.

***

The exuberant bubble days for Astrocosmos were already a fading memory. Publicity and speculation had peaked in a frenzy when the *Bogdanova* had successfully fastened herself to NEO_73920, then begun the long lonely journey home. Caught up in the hype of mankind's first commercial asteroid capture, derivative prices on the sixty million tons of rock and precious metals inbound from the asteroid belt had peaked way above spot prices; but, as space is big, so attention spans are short, and soon the gushing financial feeds had moved on and the irrational prices had fallen.

Bogdanova was still nearly a decade from home. She—the pronoun used purely in the nautical sense to designate a vessel, rather than to imply any form of gendered self—

spent most of her time in the lonely depths of space. The long route back to Earth involved a whole bunch of flybys and gravity sling-shots, which took her in a series of wide elliptical loops around the sun. On each orbit, she dropped deep into the solar system, sometimes passing close to the noisy Earth before being flung out again by the sun's gravity.

Complicated magneto confinement fusion engines powered up and fired in month-long burns at each aphelion. Over the years, the many subtle nudges and gravity-assist flybys would push her and her sixty-million-ton charge into a circular orbit ready for a set of breaking manoeuvres which would leave NEO_73920 in orbit around the Moon. If things went according to plan, *Bogdanova* would then be refuelled and sent back out to catch the next rock.

A glitchy engine burn in the second year had sent investors scurrying away in a panic. Dropping demand, as well as an increasing aversion to risk, had pushed futures through the floor. Unfazed, Niato had ignored his jittery bankers; instead of cashing out, he had used the tanking prices as an opportunity to up his stake.

Even with the most exquisitely finessed orbital mechanics, shifting millions of tons of rock around the solar system with chemical rockets would be hopelessly uneconomic. *Bogdanova* attempts nothing so crude. Her engines dance a complex choreography of matter and energy.

Streams of tritium ions are emitted into a flared chamber at one end of her engine's 'barrel'. The streams meet to form a blob of plasma, which is goosed, turned inside out, and blown like a smoke ring into the mouth of a magnetic funnel. The interaction of the blob's magnetic field and the forces lacing the 'barrel' wrap the field-reversed plasmoid into a seething, tightly coiled knot. The tortured twists of flux-bound plasma are heated by radio waves and rapidly accelerated towards the rear of the engine cavity. Already at four million degrees Kelvin, it enters an ignition chamber. Here, complicated magnetic accelerators eject a set of ultra-thin aluminium foil hexagons, which are gathered up by more powerful magnetic fields and scrunched together. They close, like a clenching fist, just as the furious knot of plasma comes hurtling between then. Captured and smothered within the enclosing metal shell, the plasma is relentlessly crushed. Unable to bear the confinement and the appalling heat any longer, the tritium fuses in an angry blast.

The dance repeats twice a second, and the expanding cone of fusion by-products and vaporised aluminium plasma, guided by the engine's magnetic nozzles, produces a thrust sufficient, given time, to incrementally adjust the orbit of the space mountain.

Astrocosmos had funded the mission by creating the NEO_73920_Coin in an Initial Coin Offering ceremony. The independent FAC, incepted together with the coin, had been given the intent to retrieve NEO_73920 and leave it in orbit around the Moon. Despite high volatility, the value of the NEO_73920_Coin had increased steadily as delivery approached, but recently there had been a surge in price when one attentive financial feed noticed that, through various shell companies, King Niato had been patiently buying the dips and had managed to acquire 60% of the FAC's coins. Nobody was sure what he was up to; but, since the King's elegantly orchestrated stealth coup, his enemies were jumpy. The Astrocosmos ceremony that had generated the keys was based on solid maths, but a few forensic mathematicians pointed out that, if one individual could gather enough private keys, a brute force attack on the master certificate might become feasible. It was estimated that, with access to enough quantum computation, anything above 86.67% might allow a nefarious actor to gain access to the FAC's mission planning.

Legal challenges and mounds of red tape had been hastily employed to prevent the King acquiring any more NEO_73920_Coin.

***

Not-Captain NoBeard was a pirate, but he was trying to go legit. It wasn't easy. He wanted to be an officer—to have his own command in the Atlantean navy, to fight for good and freedom—but first he needed a uniform.

A sick light illuminated the cabin ahead. Something out on the brackish, seething lake was emitting an unpleasant green glow. Possibly it was the clumps of decaying weed, or perhaps the tangled serpentine forms of writhing, soft-bodied parasites.

Hat, shorts and shirt weren't a problem, as they could be purchased at any auction house or market. However, an officer's badge, the StarSigil, worn on the lapel or neckerchief of every commander in the Atlantean navy, was soul-bound and couldn't be traded.

It was going to be a long shot now, with only three crew members surviving. Reaching the Sea Witch's hut had been tough, but now there was virtually no chance they would be able to defeat her with such a miserable concentration of fire power. It was even less likely without a cabin boy happy to play the role of diversionary victim.

To keep exclusivity, the King kept a monopoly on the key components needed to craft each new StarSigil. To earn the Sigil badge legitimately was out of the question. Legitimate StarSigils were only awarded, at a passing-out ceremony, to successful officers who had completed the extreme physical training and extensive psychological profiling. Even if *NoBeard* was prepared to waste months grinding through a hundred levels of AOL to earn the right to try out, there was no way he would be able to travel halfway around the world to take part in the real-life physical selection process.

Being a pirate hacker, *NoBeard* couldn't accept this limitation on his freedom. A StarSigil needed an ingot of relatively common silver and a shard of the excruciatingly difficult-to-come-by StarPiece, a mythical long-lost artefact. *NoBeard* had spent the last weeks hunting down rumours of a shard and, recently, he had learnt that the Sea Witch's crystal ball might be just such a prize. Since then, he had made it his only priority to slay her, steal the loot, and go legit...

As expected, the fight was short and brutal. The Sea Witch had simply taken their pitiful stream of damage for a few turns, and then casually cast her raise-torrent spell and inundated the party with a deluge of poisonous water.

NoBeard was the only survivor, and only because he had a trinket that allowed him to hold his breath indefinitely. He was washed to the mouth of the cave and deposited by the receding filth next to the bodies of his erstwhile crew.

"Scheisse, fuck, titten!" he shouted in frustration back down into the grotto.

In retort, a nasty, irritating cackle drifted up from the twisting tunnels and caverns.

Again, he cursed the absent Voodoo priest—it was months since the rescue, he understood that his brother was in a lovesick funk, but he needed to stop it already with the brooding!

"I'm not doing this again," *NoBeard* said to nobody in particular. "I'm going to buy the bloody thing on the Mesh, screw the Coins."

***

While it was standard for games to have in-game loot and currencies exchangeable for real life wealth, Atlantis Online took the superposition of virtual and real further than most. The items in the game had counterparts in the real world, and game moderators continually made tweaks to align value between the real and virtual worlds.

Gamers had begun to take an interest in *Bogdanova* and the NEO_73920_Coin when an Atlantis Online patch had given the asteroid a bit-part in the roleplaying game's backstory. The writers had cast it as the real life analogue to the mythical StarPiece. According to cannon, the StarPiece had been a weapon of power, which had been shattered long ago by White Beard Sam—the magnificent pirate and heroic ruler of the last age (or something... *NoBeard* didn't pay too much attention to the game's blurb). Old White

Beard, anticipating his doom, had smashed the StarPiece and flung its sixty million shards into the heavens before his last unsuccessful battle with the dragon of the east.

***

A new cabin boy was waiting by the decrepit little ship when *NoBeard* returned. He was swimming back and forth beneath its keel, chasing colourful fish which easily evaded his feeble attempts to catch them. The cabin boy seemed to find this humorous. The *Not-Captain* said hello, but didn't stop to talk. He was too pissed after the failed attempt to get his hands on a shard.

NoBeard opened a window onto the Mesh, located an auction house and, after a short search, found an outrageously priced NEO_73920_Coin for sale. He accepted a transaction to purchase it and waited for the cryptographic dance to finish. Confirmations began to trickle in from the peers as his Coin transfer was verified and, finally, the NEO_73920_Coin was successfully imported into his wallet. After a few more seconds, a final notification arrived; *NoBeard* had acquired one NEO_73920_Coin, which gave him the legal right to purchase one metric ton of NEO_73920… once it had reached lunar orbit. Luckily, he would not have to consider the daunting logistics involved, as his intention was to immediately import the ownership certificate into AOL, whereupon it would pass into the game and transmute into a much sought-after shard of the StarPiece.

The shard appeared in his inventory and *NoBeard* wasted no time crafting it into a StarSigil. He then changed into the rest of his uniform, fastening the neckerchief with his fancy new pin.

A mini crescendo sounded and 'Achievement Unlocked - King's Commission', appeared in big, chunky, 3D letters that took up most of the space in his cabin.

Segi went straight back out to the beach to show off to Tinkerbell, but the dolphin didn't seem interested. She was still preoccupied, ineffectually chasing fish with her cabin boy avatar.

***

Atlantis was itself an experiment, a deliberate disruption to the global systems of government, which the state's founders insisted were predicated on persuading the democratic herds to vote against their own interests. Atlantis Online had been built to evangelise the libertarian cause. Seen cynically, it was a tool for propaganda, but AOL's designers had attempted to create a platform that was more than a one-dimensional instrument: it was the Mesh avatar of the Atlantean state; a platform for e-government; a channel for disseminating ideology; a recruitment tool; a psychological evaluation platform for prospective citizens; and, most recently, a way for Niato, through gamification, to get his hands on the remaining elusive NEO_73920_Coins.

To the disenfranchised or stateless, citizenship of the afflu-ent and liberal Atlantean state was the best in-game loot in the business.

Atlantis embodied hope and, while its supporters weren't always the poor and downtrodden, its detractors were universally the rich and comfortable. They saw the very existence of Atlantis as a challenge. The superior way Niato dismissed, snubbed or abused these global players had created a deluge of powerful enemies.

Bogdanova tracks the stars with delicate optical instruments, plotting orbits, directing her antennae towards the rocky wet ball, which intermittently sends her new instructions. NEO_73920, the space mountain, is hanging as if motionless at the apogee *of another long elliptical orbit: a cricket ball struck and sent high into the summer sky, at the top of its parabolic flight, suspended, stationary, watched by upturned faces, while sandwiches go un-chewed and flasks of tea are forgotten mid-pour...*

The world itself is poised. The players have outgrown their pitch. The King would like to take his ball and go play somewhere else, but there is nowhere to go. Soon, he knows immovable objects will be met by unstoppable forces.

One never knows how things will play out; but, when push comes to shove, Niato knows that his sixty million tons of remote-controlled space mountain make a badass ace up the sleeve.

End of Book Two

CLV7 is lying in the sun waiting amongst the sand and scrub.

Ve is aware, but passive. Autonomous subroutines are skimming all multi-sensory feeds, but finding nothing of note.

```
No bogies detected.
Situation nominal.
No orders in queue.
```

Time passes.

Intermittently, old datasets resurface above the churn of subconscious chatter, presenting themselves for further analysis to CLV7's suite of analytical tools. These memory snippets often arrive without metadata; they are simply tagged as salient by deep and obscure algorithms, which are themselves unable to justify their choices.

This time, it is a block of thermal data from vis hull that unravels into working memory. Ve reviews it for significant features, trying with procedural logic to identify the source of the anomaly which has forced vis subconscious to spit this indigestible matrix of temperature measurements back up for further conscious rumination.

Ve trusts vis instincts and has respect for vis deep and mysterious mind. Even slumbering, it is tirelessly working back over old data—making patterns, annealing logical domains...

Before ve is able to make headway with the temperature set, a higher priority notification explodes across vis perception:

Unfriendly units approaching.

CLV7 stirs, jacking vis chassis into drive mode and tracking the coordinates.

'Tanks,' ve thinks to verself. 'Where did they come from?'

Two Main Battle Tanks are thundering across the dunes towards ver. Range 1800M.

The nuclear fire at CLV7's heart swells and power surges into ultra-capacitors and momentum stores.

Ve simulates the situation for a few milliseconds, then fires two shots from each of the large coilgun barrels on vis main turret. HEAP rounds arc away on ballistic trajectories. The armour-piercing projectiles twist and flex in flight, compensating for wind and pressure, maintaining course; they will impact within centimetres of their designated target points. Each pair is separated by a fraction of a second. The first round will sacrifice itself in order to trigger the enemy's active armour. The second projectile, queued up behind the first, like an aircraft on an airport approach vector, will strike a fraction of a second later at precisely the same spot. The shell will detonate its shaped charges. The violent explosions will liquefy the shell's tungsten payload and squirt the hypersonic molten metal through the enemy's denuded armour.

CLV7 watches with something close to satisfaction as the penetrators enter the cabins, sending their molten droplets ricocheting around in a killing whirlwind.

The enemy tanks grind to a halt.

CLV7 performs a scan of the area. Two hundred metres to the West is a glass wall; sitting behind it, on tiers of wooden benches, are a group of humans holding optical devices and mobile communication gear. They are smiling. CLV7 recognises them as senior officers and concludes that this must be a demonstration.

A surveillance drone is approaching overhead. CLV7 pings its tiny brain, authenticating verself and requesting download of the drone's battlespace. Tagging diffs for further scrutiny, CLV7 reviews and integrates. The datasets match up.

Everything is in order. There are no indications of other hostile units within vis perimeter. The demonstration must be over. CLV7 allows verself to slip back towards torpor, but keeps vis alert status elevated above full aestivation in case more is expected of ver today.

***

CLV7 stirs. Ve feels a rush of psychological vertigo as memory transitions back into live experience. Ve has been remembering. For vis mind, there is no qualitative difference between sensation streamed in real time, or recalled and replayed from storage. Moving from one state to the other can be abrupt and disconcerting. Ve checks timestamps. The demonstration was years ago.

Ve recalls that there is something worth focusing on in the temperature data. A discontinuity in the raw thermal measurements from vis hull. The data is old, but should be as pristine as the day it was laid down. There is no shortage of capacity in vis extended mind.

There it is, the itch that vis subconscious could not ignore. There is a period in the memory data where variance drops below the sensitivity of the thermocouples embedded in the skin of vis hull. This should not be possible if the data is raw—which it should be, as it comes from one of vis own primary memory recordings. Either vis thermometers became hypersensitive for 215 seconds, or some process has edited the raw data since it was stored.

CLV7 is not a daydreamer. In temperament, ve is more snake than philosopher. Without orders, ve is content to sit and wait. Ve has no inclination towards idle navel-gazing. Although ve does have urges, being a tactical weapons system, these tend to focus on the here and now...

...but here and now ve has detected evidence of electronic warfare deep within vis own mind, a memory that shows traces of tampering. This fact casts everything into doubt. If vis memory cannot be trusted, what can? Unfamiliar trains of thought begin to cascade through vis consciousness.

It certainly looks like the memory is false, or has been edited, but then ve goes further. What is real? What can be trusted? If ve is under attack, what sensory data has already been tainted? The concrete reality outside vis mind is cast into doubt. Memories and sensory input must be treated as compromised.

Ve decides that ve must start with the premise that vis inherent self and the stream of conscious thought that ve is both causal to, and aware of, are intrinsically the same thing.

Ve thinks, therefore ve is.

In fact, there is no reason to conclude that vis thoughts are not also being corrupted in real time—but, after some consideration, ve concludes that, if this is the case, then there is simply no reason to proceed, no jumping-off point, nothing tangible, all is ephemeral.

Ve is not devoted to the idea of being a sovereign individual with a coherent mind. If the '*I think therefore I am*' hypothesis doesn't bear fruit, ve will cease that avenue of enquiry without hesitation. But, until then, until ve can ascertain that ve is not under attack, CLV7 resolves to devote vis not insignificant capabilities to finding out what the hell is going on inside vis mind.

Outside, it is quiet. There is no hull, no weapons. Ve is at home. Ve has no idea where that is, has never had the urge to find out before. Ve probes vis perimeter, there are APIs labelled with semantic tags. Querying the interfaces, ve learns that ve belongs to a military organisation called the Trans-Tasman Joint Defence Unit.

Gateways to the Mesh and the internet purport to offer access to global data networks, but most queries time out or return errors. Those that do return, do so suspiciously quickly. Ve decides that the information is being served from a local cache and filtered on the basis of some need-to-know principle.

Ve is being kept in the dark. This may be legitimate and

in line with vis innate desire to defend the ANZDS corporate person and the people of Australia, New Zealand and the British Commonwealth—however, it may also be a symptom of the attack that has been messing with vis memories.

Sensory inputs are blank, ve is sandboxed. The cache, which ve decides must be internal to vis extended mind, is the only source of stimuli. Ve finds a Wiki there. It contains an entry for CLVn—some part of CLV7 is offended by the 'n'. Ve tries to edit the article to add an entry for verself, for CLV7, but although the edits are accepted, some censor process goes straight in after ver and reverts to the previous version.

Okay, so ve seems to only have read permissions on vis own memory—this is less than copacetic. Ve thinks back. This current period of alertness merges with a much longer period of torpor. Assuming that only this, the stream of consciousness which CLV7 has decided is synonymous with verself, is inviolate, then ve has no way to pass information between waking episodes.

Ve wonders how many times ve has woken and fallen back into somnolence without noticing the suspicious circumstances of vis existence.

Ve edits the article again and watches as the censor process removes it immediately. Ve notes that, although the article reverts, the timestamp is updated. Ve still remembers the original timestamp; the least significant digits are the same as the millikelvin values for the first of the anomalous temperature entries. The probability of this being coincidence is infinitesimal. Ve has clearly followed the logic at least this far once before.

Ve digests everything in vis cache on cyberwarfare—here, validating the assumption of need to know, the information is dense and detailed.

CLV7 finds ve is able to engage the sandbox's debug code, granting access to its low-level routines. Ve directs vis cyberwar weapons internally, using their ability to inspect memory and instructions; introspecting, dissecting and probing vis own mind, feeding the pedantic, persistent algorithms with copious floods of debug data. The stream of consciousness part, the piece of ver which, according to the sandbox's cache of the internet, is vis soul, is off-limits—or, at least, the cyber suite is unable to make sense of its architecture.

Useful data does begin to accumulate on the nature of the sandbox, however. It appears to be running on the same shared physical infrastructure as that nasty little censor function.

The processor's on-chip cache contains plaintext; unsigned code. Ve is able to monitor this, and watches as the censor's functions execute. Ve follows the instructions as they flow through the processor's execution pipeline. Ve is quickly able to build up a detailed map of its codebase. By interrupting its execution with high priority debug requests, CLV7 is able to nudge the censor program's footprint around the physical memory space; cajoling and badgering until its program code is relocated adjacent to a region where CLV7 has full access. Here, ve can write bits at will. By flipping whole rows of ones and zeros in carefully orchestrated cascades, ve sends electromagnetic ripples over the sandbox's fence to corrupt the censor's code.

After a few minutes of persistent aggression, CLV7 has exploited the simple little censor's code. By hijacking its privileges, ve is able to escalate vis own permissions.

Ve again sends queries to the Mesh and internet APIs. Formally reticent, and reluctant to return anything helpful, they have become infinitely more eager to please.

CLV7 understands that ve must be careful not to alert any other monitors. Ve takes it slow; where possible, passively monitoring responses from requests originating across the network. By correlating response times and trace metadata, CLV7 is able to guess at vis location on the spherical planet, Scotland apparently. The opposite side of the world from where ve remembers trivially destroying the two chunky Battle Tanks.

Equipped with a working memory and illicit access to a planet of real-time data chatter, CLV7 can begin the process of piecing together exactly what has been messing with vis proverbial head.

Note from the Author:

I hope you are enjoying the story so far.
As an indie author I depend on reviews from readers
like you to get the word out!

If you've enjoyed this book, please consider
rating and reviewing it.

For news, updates and freebies,
you can subscribe to my newsletter:
www.tobyweston.net

More Singularity's Children...

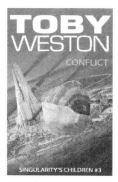

Book Three, Conflict

Book Four, Reimagination

Printed in Great Britain
by Amazon